The Right-Under Club

ALSO BY CHRISTINE HURLEY DERISO

Do-Over

The Right-Under Club

christine hurley deriso

delacorte press

Published by Delacorte Press
an imprint of Random House Children's Books
a division of Random House, Inc.
New York

www.randomhouse.com/kids

Educators and librarians, for a variety of teaching tools, visit us at
www.randomhouse.com/teachers

Library of Congress Cataloging-in-Publication Data

Deriso, Christine Hurley.
The Right-Under Club / Christine Hurley Deriso.—1st ed.
p. cm.
Summary: Over the summer, five middle school girls form a club based on the fact that they all feel neglected and misunderstood by their blended families.
ISBN-13: 978-0-385-73334-2 (trade)—ISBN-13: 978-0-385-90351-6 (glb)
[1. Clubs—Fiction. 2. Stepfamilies—Fiction. 3. Family problems—Fiction. 4. Friendship—Fiction.] I. Title.
PZ7.D4427Ri 2007
[Fic]—dc22
2006019768

The text of this book is set in 12-point Goudy.

Book design by Kenny Holcomb

Printed in the United States of America

10 9 8 7 6 5 4 3 2 1

First Edition

To Jules, my "editor" who keeps it real.
I love you.

1

"*Mine!*"

At age twelve, Tricia was a little old for one-word sentences screamed at the top of her lungs, but ever since her half sister had reached the terrible twos, brattiness had seemed contagious in the household.

Tricia swished her straight blond hair out of her face, squinted, clenched her teeth and turned bright red in her effort to wrest her CD from her little sister's chubby hands.

"*Mine!*" Tricia repeated to her sister.

"*Mine!*" Hissy squealed in protest, tugging harder on the CD.

"*Mom!*" Tricia wailed.

"Just let her have it, Tricia!" their mom called wearily from the kitchen.

"Oh, I'll let her have it, all right!"

"*Hey!* Enough with the attitude!" her mom barked.

"Doesn't 'attitude' need an adjective?" Tricia snarled, this time more to herself than to her mom. What was the point?

She relaxed her grip on the CD and leaned into Hissy's face with slitted, menacing eyes. "Hisssssss!" she said, a snake imitation that usually reduced her little sister to tears.

Not this time. Hissy poked out her bottom lip. "Meanie!" She spun on a bare heel and toddled off indignantly with Tricia's CD.

Tricia rolled her eyes and plopped backward onto her bed. Little sisters were so exasperating. "Hissy's a brat!" she called out to no one in particular.

"Don't call your sister a brat!" her mom called back. "And don't call her Hissy!"

There were lots of reasons Tricia called her sister Hissy. She had written them down in her journal:

She has hissy fits at least a thousand times a day.
Saying it gives me a chance to hiss at her (which she hates).
It's short for half sis.
Hissy is HIS daughter. (Mom's, too, of course. But HIS. Hisssss.)
Hissy's real name, Everly, is just too ridiculous. (HE made it up.)
"Hissy" gets me in less trouble than my other nickname for her: Neverly.

Tricia flopped over and buried her face in her solar system bedspread. "Grrrrr!" She rubbed her forehead against Pluto.

"What did she take this time?" her mom asked. Tricia turned onto her side and saw her mom standing in the bedroom doorway holding a dish towel.

"What hasn't she taken of mine?" Tricia groaned. "She destroys everything I own."

Her mom laughed lightly, then walked over and tousled Tricia's hair. "Hey, you used to be two," she said, "and believe it or not, you were a lot like her."

With their heart-shaped face and the single dimple in their

left cheek, Tricia couldn't deny how much she and Everly looked alike. But they certainly didn't act alike. As if.

Her mom seemed to read her mind. "You were just as stubborn as Everly." She swatted the dish towel playfully against Tricia's legs. "Still are."

"But I didn't have a big sister to torment."

"Right," her mom agreed. "Only me."

"And Dad," Tricia said petulantly.

Her mom bit her bottom lip. "Right. And Dad."

It was a sore subject. Tricia's mom kept trying to erase her dad from their lives, and Tricia kept trying to pencil him back in.

"Quit being so crabby," her mom said, smoothing Tricia's hair. "A new house, your own room . . . you're not quite as pitiful as you make yourself out to be."

Right . . . a new house. True, it was much bigger than their old one, and thank heaven she no longer had to share a room with Hissy. But *he* picked it out, so how could it ever really feel like home? The neighborhood had a hoity-toity guardhouse at the entrance and lawns that looked so perfect, a stray dandelion on a bright green carpet of grass was liable to trigger a frantic call to 911. The houses looked like museums, with white columns in front and ceilings so high that your voice echoed.

"It doesn't feel much like home," Tricia mumbled to her mom.

"Give it time," her mom said soothingly. "We just moved in three days ago. I've already seen tons of girls your age riding their bikes. By the time you start your new school this fall, you'll already have made loads of new friends. I guarantee it."

By now, Hissy had toddled back in and walked over to Tricia's bed. Her face broke into a rose-petal smile as she extended a pudgy arm and handed the CD back to her big sister. "A present!" the little girl cooed.

Tricia grinned in spite of herself as she sat up on the bed and took the CD. "Thanks for the 'present,' " she said, then grimaced and wiped a damp hand on her shorts. "And thanks for drooling all over it. I'm sure it'll sound much better that way."

She playfully pinched Everly's cheek. The kid was so annoying. But Tricia loved her anyhow. It was one of many paradoxes in her life right now. She had written them in her journal:

I love having my own room. I hated moving.
I love that Mom and Dad don't fight much anymore. I hate that they got a divorce.
I loved helping Mom plan her wedding. I hate that she got remarried.
I love visiting Dad. I hate that I have to visit Dad, because that's what you do with uncles, not dads. Dads are supposed to live with you.
I love that Mom has new people in her life to love. I hate having to share her.
I love that I'm almost a teenager. I hate being twelve.

"Why don't you read Everly a story while I finish the lunch dishes?" her mom said, tossing the dish towel over her shoulder and walking back toward the kitchen.

Tricia grumbled. "Let's cut to the chase," she said to her sister, who was already cuddling into her lap. "Everybody lived happily ever after. Or, in your case, they lived happily Everly after."

"Book!" Everly demanded, so Tricia sighed, reached across her bed and grabbed *Cinderella*, Everly's favorite, from her bedside table. Everly called it "Umberella." Tricia turned to the first page.

"Once upon a time, there lived a girl named . . ."

She always paused at this part.

"Umberella," Everly said, filling in the word on cue.

"Umberella," Tricia repeated, kissing the top of her sister's silky head. Then she improvised. "See, Umberella had everything going for her until her dad hooked up with some new family, at which point Umberella turned into the leftover meat loaf somebody puts in the back of the refrigerator and forgets all about until the meat loaf starts stinking up the place, at which point everybody hates the meat loaf, as if it's the meat loaf's fault that everybody forgot about it and it turned all stinky."

"Umberella," Everly repeated contentedly, flipping to the back of the book so she could see her favorite picture of Cinderella transformed into a beautiful princess.

"Right," Tricia muttered. "And they all lived happily Everly after."

2

"You're going out like that?"

Twelve-year-old Hope's bright blue eyes narrowed as she stopped in her tracks on her way toward the front door. "Like what?"

Hope's stepmother, Jacie, waved a hand through the air, aiming for casual as she stood in the foyer subtly inspecting her rumpled stepdaughter. "Oh, nothing. It's just . . . your hair's a little messy."

Hope tried to feign indifference, but she self-consciously tucked an unruly copper-colored ringlet behind her ear.

"Your hair looks fine," Hope's best friend, Mei, said gently. Hope loved Mei for being supportive; she'd been loyal to the core since they met four summers earlier, when Hope had moved into the neighborhood. But Hope couldn't help feeling a twinge of envy. Mei's glossy black hair framed her delicate Asian features beautifully. Why couldn't Hope have sleek, straight hair? And why was Jacie constantly rubbing it in her face that she didn't?

"Where are you girls going, anyhow?" Jacie asked, eager

to change the subject and defuse her supersensitive stepdaughter's irritation.

"Just out," Hope replied tersely.

"We thought we'd bum around the neighborhood for a while," Mei said with a smile. It was true that Jacie's "constructive" criticism wore a little thin, but Mei thought she was a nice lady who tried awfully hard. And the things Hope most disliked about her stepmother—her fine blond hair, her dainty nose, her ultrafeminine flair—were beyond her control anyhow. It wasn't fair for Hope to despise Jacie for being pretty. But she did. Mei always felt torn when she was around them . . . Jacie trying so hard, yet always managing to say the wrong thing . . . Hope never giving her the benefit of the doubt, yet with often understandably hurt feelings. They were both great people. But they weren't great together. Kind of like Mei and her stepfather, Stan. A lot like that, actually.

"Aren't you supposed to be tutoring Leighton now?" Jacie asked Hope.

Hope rolled her eyes. "She stood me up. Again."

Hope and her thirteen-year-old neighbor, Leighton, had nothing in common except that they were both going to be eighth graders at Clearview Middle School. Academics had never been Leighton's strong suit, and when she joined the cheerleading squad in seventh grade, schoolwork fell completely off her radar screen. Hope's natural intelligence combined with her mind-of-their-own ringlets sealed her fate as Clearview Middle School's official nerd—the polar opposite of gorgeous, too-cool Leighton. When Leighton's mom had asked Hope to tutor her daughter in math over the summer,

Hope had been less than optimistic—and less than thrilled—at the prospect of spending so much time with the biggest snob in school. No big surprise that Leighton had blown off the first two sessions.

"Did you call her?" Jacie asked, looking concerned.

"Duh," Hope said. "Her mom answered the phone and said, 'I thought she was at your house.' "

Mei laughed lightly at Hope's breathy imitation of Leighton's clueless mother.

"Maybe she's on her way over," Jacie said.

"Or maybe not," Hope replied. "Considering she should've been here forty minutes ago, I'm thinking not."

Jacie's eyebrows furrowed. "I really hope the tutoring works out," she said. "I'd love for you to get to know Leighton better. She seems like such a nice girl."

Hope and Mei exchanged glances, and Mei forced herself not to smile. There were lots of ways to describe Leighton, but "nice girl" didn't make the cut.

"C'mon, Mei," Hope said, reaching for the doorknob. "We're outie."

"Bye," Mei said to Jacie, then followed her friend out the front door.

Hope made a point of slamming the front door with a flourish, then shook her head as she and Mei walked down the driveway. " 'She seems like such a nice girl,' " she said, imitating Jacie. " 'And maybe if you hang around her, dear, you can pick up some beauty tips.' "

Mei gave her friend a playful push. "Your poor stepmother," she said. "She can't win with you."

Hope shrugged, holding the palms of her hands skyward.

"Duh. You can't exactly win with a loser, now, can you, Einstein?"

But her tone was light, and a warm breeze blew the smell of jasmine in their direction. Hope took a deep breath. True, Jacie was totally annoying. But on a warm summer day with her best friend by her side, how bad could things be?

3

Beeeeep!

Pedestrians were so annoying.

Leighton adjusted her sunglasses and floored the accelerator of her golf cart. The pedestrian she almost nailed shot her an icy glare, but Leighton had already moved on. Funny that she was in a hurry, considering she was going exactly nowhere, but that never slowed her down. She tossed her head jauntily, her thick brown hair flowing behind her like a wave.

"You act like you rule the universe," her stepbrother, Kyle, had told her once.

"Trust me: if I did, you'd be long gone," she'd replied.

True, she had nowhere to go on this hot June afternoon, but since summer vacation had started a week earlier, Leighton had been having serious issues with personal space. Kyle was barely tolerable during the school year, but at least they had separate teachers. (Kyle was in all the brainiac classes.) Having to deal with him 24–7 at home was going to make for a very long summer. Thank God she'd finally worn down her mom and stepdad, convincing them that if she didn't have her own golf cart, she'd just die. Of course, now that she had one, she was thinking what she really needed was a BlackBerry so she could IM her friends from wherever she escaped to. Give her a week . . . two weeks tops. She'd wear 'em down. She always did.

It wasn't that she was spoiled. "So the opposite," she said with a sniff to her friends when they leveled the accusation. She and her mom had been downright poor all those years they'd lived together, just the two of them, in one tiny apartment or duplex after another. Leighton hadn't been thrilled when her mom remarried a year earlier (hello, nerdy Kyle came with the package), but at least her stepdad, Carl, was rich, compared to what she was used to. No more shopping at those tacky outlet stores for irregulars or off-season clearance items. Trendy clothes and a golf cart were the least she deserved, putting up with a loser stepbrother who was only one month older and in the very same grade.

"That's your brother?" people had asked her constantly during seventh grade as he ambled toward his locker, all gangly arms and knobby knees.

"Step," she would quickly clarify. "Totally separate gene pool." As if it wasn't, like, so obvious. Leighton was the prettiest girl at Clearview Middle School (simply a fact . . . everybody said so) and Kyle was the dorkiest guy. Just her luck that their parents had met at the school's open house two years earlier and had made like lovesick teenagers ever since. The wedding was nothing short of mortifying, with gawky Kyle adjusting the fly of his tuxedo while he walked Leighton down the aisle.

"Would you stop it!" she'd spat under her breath, not yet having learned that Kyle was hopeless, a lost cause, a poster child for dweebs, with his black-rimmed glasses and show-off vocabulary. Leighton was the coolest kid in middle school, but even she couldn't redeem Kyle. The most she could hope for was to avoid him. Without this golf cart, she'd be sunk. Now all she needed was a BlackBerry. . . .

Beeeeeep!

Leighton slammed on her brakes. Some moron on a skateboard had just whizzed directly into the path of the golf cart. The horn apparently startled the skateboarder, who veered too sharply, then crashed onto the sidewalk in a heap.

"You okay?" Leighton asked hesitantly, too irritated from the disruption to feign much concern.

"I'm fine," the skateboarder said, standing up and brushing damp grass off her legs. She was annoyed, too. It was the golf cart that had come tearing into her path, not the other way around.

"I'm Tricia," the skateboarder said.

Leighton curled her lip and pushed her sunglasses onto the top of her head, revealing ocean green eyes. "Yeah, well . . . I'm outta here," she said, preparing to zoom off again.

"Where ya headed?" Tricia asked, more out of boredom than curiosity.

Leighton raised an eyebrow. "Around," she said coolly.

Tricia rolled her eyes. So much for her mother's guarantee of "loads of friends" in her new neighborhood. "Yeah, well, see ya," she replied, then righted her skateboard and prepared to hop back on.

"Uh . . . ," Leighton said hesitantly.

"Yes?"

"My name's Leighton." She smoothed a lock of hair with the heel of her hand.

Tricia's face grudgingly softened into a smile. "Hi, Leighton. I just moved into the neighborhood three days ago."

"Where are you headed?" Leighton asked, trying to sound uninterested.

Tricia shrugged. "Nowhere. Just trying to escape. If I stayed home, I'd be stuck reading "Cinderella" to my little sister for the fiftieth time in a row."

Leighton giggled and held fingertips with manicured nails against her lips. "I'm escaping, too. My dweeby stepbrother."

"What's his name?" Tricia asked, nudging the skateboard lazily back and forth with her foot.

"Kyle. Kyle Clayton. Ugggh."

Tricia brightened. "Hey, I know a Kyle Clayton. Did he go to Northside Elementary School?"

Leighton rolled her eyes. "Yeah."

"Me too. He was in my third-grade class. Isn't he, like, a genius?"

"Whatever." Leighton sniffed.

"He's funny, too," Tricia said. "He said such off-the-wall things in class. He was always making us laugh."

"Yeah, he's a regular riot," Leighton said, then pulled a tube of lipstick from the pocket of her low-rise shorts and slowly circled her full, peach-colored lips. She smacked them together and returned the lipstick tube to her pocket.

"You wear lipstick already?" Tricia asked in a tone that Leighton wasn't sure was admiring or disapproving.

"Duh," she responded. "Since like sixth grade."

"What grade are you in now?"

"I'm going into eighth. I know: you're thinking I look like I'm in high school."

"Ohh-kay." Tricia resisted the urge to snicker.

"Everybody thinks that," Leighton continued breezily. "High school seniors have asked me out."

Now, that was pretty impressive. "Does your mom let you date them?" Tricia asked.

Leighton leaned closer with a conspiratorial smile. "Not yet. But I'm thinking this is the year I wear her down. There's a hottie named Scott who I am totally crushing on."

"Well, good luck with that," Tricia said in a playful tone. True, Leighton was a snob, but Tricia was more amused than irritated. And at least Miss All That was talking to her. Beggars couldn't be choosers.

"Wanna come to my house?" Tricia sucked in her breath a little as soon as the words had impulsively tumbled from her mouth. It was probably a stupid thing to say. Leighton didn't seem like a come-over-and-play type of girl.

Leighton eyed her steadily before responding, then lowered her sunglasses. Tricia had no idea what she would say.

"Okay."

That was it. Just . . . "Okay."

"Okay," Tricia responded nervously. Now that the Beauty Queen had agreed to come over, what would she do with her? Offer her a pedicure? Dusting off the Easy-Bake Oven seemed totally out of the question.

"Put your skateboard in the back and hop on," Leighton said.

Tricia tossed a lock of blond hair over her shoulder and followed the instructions. It felt weird to actually be sitting in one of these things. She'd seen them all over the neighborhood. They seemed so silly. Tricia hated any whiff of snobbishness, and golf carts stank to high heaven. Now she was in a snobby golf cart with the snobbiest girl she'd ever met.

Leighton floored the accelerator, and Tricia clutched the bar to keep from tipping onto the street. "Hey!" Tricia yelped. It was hard to play it cool when you felt like hurling.

"Chill!" Leighton demanded. "So which way to your house?"

"Uh . . . take a right here," Tricia said, then tightened her grip as Leighton jerked the steering wheel, sending the golf cart screeching down her street.

"Leighton! You're gonna make me barf!" Tricia moaned. By now, coolness was out of the question. Her only priority was getting to her house without leaving body parts strewn in the street.

"Like, get a life, girl!" Leighton said, but she was laughing.

"Who taught you how to drive? Jeff Gordon?"

"Who?"

"Never mind. Just . . . Hey, watch out for those girls!"

Leighton was hurtling toward two girls walking in their direction. The girls' eyebrows arched in fear. Simultaneously, they pitched their bodies sideways in opposite directions, just in time to avoid being flattened.

"Leighton!" one of them groaned.

Leighton slammed on her brakes. "Like, hel-*lo*!" she called out. "Are you trying to make me crash?"

The girls approached the golf cart, smoothing their T-shirts.

"Next time, let us know when you'll be driving your golf cart so we can wear body armor," one of them said.

Leighton leaned toward Tricia. "They are so immature," she murmured.

"So who's your new friend?" the redhead asked.

"I'm Tricia. I just moved here three days ago."

"Three days and Leighton hasn't flattened you yet with her

new golf cart?" The girls laughed lightly. "I'm Hope, and this is Mei."

Hope eyed Leighton knowingly. "You were supposed to be at my house an hour ago for tutoring."

Leighton yawned dramatically. "Oh, that. Forgot. Hate it."

"Your mom's gonna hate it if you keep blowing me off," Hope said.

"Oooooo," Leighton said, tossing Hope a sneer. "I'm terrified."

"You wanna come over now?" Hope asked, underwhelmed by the thought but feeling too responsible not to ask.

"Can't. We're on our way to Tricia's house," Leighton said in a tone suggesting no one else was invited. Hope and Mei exchanged glances.

"Why don't you come, too?" Tricia blurted out. "Not that there's anything exciting to do at my house. In fact, I have a totally obnoxious little sister. But you can come if you want."

Hope's eyes danced with subversive delight at the thought of Leighton's being stuck with her. "Sure," she said. "We'd love to."

Leighton threw her hands in the air. "Whatever."

Hope and Mei hopped onto the rear seats of Leighton's golf cart. "Go easy, Leighton," Hope said. "I don't want to die young."

Leighton floored it and seemed to go out of her way to make the trip as jerky as possible. Thankfully, Tricia's house was right down the street. She sighed with relief as Leighton screeched into her driveway. As Mei and Hope tumbled out of their seats, Leighton whispered, "Why did you invite them?" Mei and Hope once again exchanged the look that was already becoming familiar to Tricia. They seemed to have a long history with Leighton.

Tricia stepped out of the golf cart. "Wanna watch music videos?" she suggested tentatively, hoping the activity sounded halfway sophisticated. In her old crowd, she had always been the last one to catch on to a new trend or abandon some kiddy interest. It wasn't that she was babyish; she just never seemed quite ready to move up a step when her friends did. It always made her feel a little out of the loop. It was time to shed that reputation.

Leighton was craning her neck, peering into Tricia's backyard. "What's that?" she asked, pointing to a tree house.

Tricia's heart sank. Why had Troy insisted on building her that stupid tree house? Talk about kid stuff. "Oh, that," she replied quickly. "It's . . . my sister's. She's only two, but my folks figured she'll grow into it. My dad . . . my stepdad . . . moved into the house about a month before the rest of us so I could finish seventh grade in my old school. He wanted to have the tree house ready for me . . . I mean, for my little sister . . . when we moved in."

"Cool," Mei said, leaning to one side for a better view.

Cool? Tricia sighed in relief. "We can check it out if you want," she said, trying to sound indifferent.

"Definitely!" Hope said. Tricia walked to the gate and unlatched it. The girls followed her into the backyard, which was already landscaped with plush grass that was damp from the automatic sprinklers. The ground squished beneath the girls' flip-flops.

"This is awesome!" Mei said as they approached the tree house. Troy had chosen the largest, sturdiest oak tree for the project. A spiral wood-plank stairway led about six feet up to the base of the cedar tree house. Like the steps, the house itself wrapped around the tree, with supporting planks of wood extending from the periphery of the house to the base of the tree. The girls unlatched a door held in place by a metal hook to get inside. Troy had built two windows into the façade for light, and Tricia's mom had scattered area rugs on the floor. The girls settled onto the rugs and inhaled the sweet cedar scent.

"We could sleep in here!" Hope said enthusiastically.

"It's okay," Leighton agreed grudgingly. "But what do you do in here?"

Tricia shrugged. "It would be a good place for a clubhouse." Again, she regretted the words as soon as she'd uttered them. A clubhouse? Very mature.

"A clubhouse!" Hope squealed, and Mei leaned in excitedly. Tricia made a mental note to stop trying to second-guess her new friends.

Leighton leaned back on the heels of her hands. "A clubhouse," she repeated, then glanced disapprovingly at Hope. "But that would require a club. And it's not like we all have a lot in common." Hope and Mei exchanged "the look" once again.

"Oh, don't we, Leighton?" Hope said sarcastically. "My goal in life is to find that perfect shade of fuchsia lipstick for my complexion. That's right up your alley, right?"

Leighton sneered, but then brightened. "Hey, you could give me a couple of math tips during our club meetings, which would get my mom off my back."

Hope clutched her heart. "Oh, Leighton. I'm . . . I'm . . ." She sighed, then feigned a choked-up whisper. "I'm touched."

Mei laughed. It might be worth joining a club just to see these two go at it on a regular basis, she thought.

"Okay, so we'll have a club," Leighton said definitively. "But what kind of club will it be?"

"Well," Tricia said, "I've just met all three of you. Why don't we spend a few minutes telling each other about ourselves?"

Leighton's eyes sparkled as she warmed immediately to the idea. "Okay, I'll start," she said authoritatively. "Here's the 411 on me: Leighton Lockwood, five foot seven, a hundred and ten pounds . . ."

"Fascinating," Hope murmured.

Leighton cleared her throat and raised an eyebrow. "As I was saying: okay, my hobbies are cheerleading, dancing and gymnastics. . . . I hate school, I love cute guys and I want to move to Hollywood after high school and do makeup for movie stars. Or *be* a movie star. And someone can do my makeup." She smiled coyly and held up her palms. "That's me."

"Okay," said Tricia. "Hope, how about you?"

Hope sat up straighter and cleared her throat. "My dream is to be Miss America."

Leighton's jaw dropped and Mei giggled.

"Okay, maybe not," Hope said. "Let's try again. My name is Hope Mitchell, I'm going into eighth grade, my favorite subject is science, I want to be a paleontologist. . . ."

"Digging up dead things?" Leighton interjected with a sneer.

"Yes, Leighton," Hope said earnestly. "Sometimes I find dead things preferable to living things." Mei stifled another giggle.

"How about you, Mei?" Tricia asked. "Where are you from?"

"Two streets over," Mei responded, sounding more snappish than she intended.

Tricia blushed.

"Sorry," Mei said softly. "I get asked that a lot."

Hope squeezed Mei's knee protectively. "Mei's an amazing artist," she said.

Mei smiled shyly. "Not really. Art's just the only thing I'm even halfway good at."

"Not true," Hope said. "She's good at lots of things, but especially art."

"Hmmmm . . . ," Tricia said. "Paleontology, makeup, art . . . you're right. We're all over the map."

"How about you?" Hope said. "The three of us have known each other forever. You're the one we don't know anything about. Spill it."

"So you haven't seen my biography on the A&E channel?" Tricia teased.

Leighton rolled her eyes.

"Actually, my life is spectacularly boring," Tricia said. "My dad is really cool . . . he's a guitarist in a band, not that you've ever heard of the band . . . but still, he's totally awesome. Not that it matters, considering I hardly ever see him."

"Why not?" Mei asked.

Tricia shrugged. "My mom is so uptight. She thinks she can form an instant family with her new husband . . . you know, just add water and stir . . . and Dad doesn't fit into the new family. The problem is, neither do I."

"I feel your pain," Mei said. "And I can't even get away from my stepdad at school. He's the principal."

Tricia gasped in sympathy.

"I can top you all," Leighton said. "My stepbrother is the biggest dweeb at Clearview Middle School."

"I like Kyle," Mei said quietly.

"Hel-*lo*!" Hope said. "I've got you all beat with my evil stepmother. Think Cinderella."

Tricia smiled. Umberella. The day was coming full circle. "So we've all got steps," she said, then nodded smartly. "That's it. We've all got steps."

"Your point?" Leighton asked.

"That's what we have in common. We all know what it feels like to be a leftover."

"A what?" Hope said.

"A leftover. Like the meat loaf somebody puts in the back of the refrigerator, then forgets about until it turns all stinky. That's what happens to kids when their parents divorce and start new families. They turn into leftovers."

The girls murmured knowingly, and a somber silence overtook the tree house.

"We're leftovers, even though we're right under their noses," Mei finally said.

Hope laughed, breaking the tension. "Leftovers who are right under their noses," she repeated. "Left . . . over. Right . . . under. Left, right. Over, under. Get it?"

Tricia grinned. "Girls, I think we've discovered our identity." She slapped her palms against her thighs. "Welcome to the Right-Under Club."

• • •

Tricia allowed herself to breathe a sigh of relief as she settled into bed that night. She'd gotten over a major hurdle: finding friends in her new neighborhood. True, she had just met them, but she could call them friends, right? After all, they'd formed a club. Fellow club members definitely qualified as friends. Leighton was over-the-top snobby, but Hope and Mei seemed cool. Maybe this new neighborhood would turn out okay after all. There were a few things Tricia was starting to like about it. She wrote them down in her journal:

My own room . . . duh.
A funny friend (Hope).
An exotic friend (Mei). (My bad for asking where she's from.)
A friend with a golf cart.
A new club!
Did I mention the friend with the golf cart?

Tricia laid her journal aside, turned off her lamp, pulled her covers up to her chin and drifted off to sleep.

4

Tricia was in the tree house fifteen minutes early for the first meeting of the Right-Under Club. She brought several small spiral-bound notebooks, pencils, a bag of potato chips, a large plastic bowl and a small cooler filled with soft drinks on ice. No club was official, she reasoned, without notebooks and snacks.

An unexpected pang of panic nagged at her as she settled into the tree house with her supplies. What if the girls didn't show? Her friends in the old neighborhood were notorious for coming up with huge plans that never made it past the idea stage. Maybe the Right-Under Club had already fizzled. After all, Leighton, Hope and Mei actually had lives. They weren't desperate for friends like Tricia was. Maybe they were all together now, giggling about what a loser Tricia was for actually thinking they were serious. Maybe . . . maybe . . .

"You up there?"

Tricia jumped at the sound of the voice. It was Hope, calling from below. Tricia sighed in relief. "Yeah," she called down. "Come on up." She heard the soft padding of tennis shoes on the wooden planks. The door to the tree house creaked open. Hope came in first, then Mei, then . . .

"Hi," Tricia said to a girl she didn't recognize.

"This is my cousin, Elizabeth," Hope said. "Our dads are brothers. I forgot to mention she'd be staying with us for a few weeks. She got here last night." She paused awkwardly, and Elizabeth stared at her shoes. "Can she be in the club?"

All eyes fell on Tricia. She hadn't planned on being in charge, but, well, it was her tree house, and she was the one who had brought the supplies.

"Are you qualified?" she asked Elizabeth with a sudden air of authority.

Elizabeth, a skinny girl with glasses and dark blond hair that tumbled in loose curls onto her shoulders, looked terrified. "What are the qualifications?" she asked in a small voice.

"Good question," said Tricia, who was itching to fill up her notebook. "I'll write them down." She turned to the first page. "QUALIFICATIONS," she wrote at the top. "Okay, first of all, you definitely have to be a girl," she said. "But you look a little young. How old are you?"

"Eleven," Elizabeth said, her eyes widening in suspense as she pondered whether the answer was acceptable.

Tricia furrowed her brow and tapped the pencil eraser against her head. "A sixth grader?" she asked.

Elizabeth nodded anxiously. "I'm starting middle school this fall."

Tricia scribbled in her notebook.

"Now for the most important question," she said, holding the eraser to her bottom lip as she stared at Elizabeth. "Are you a Right-Under?"

Elizabeth smiled broadly. Her cousin had prepared her for this one. "My parents are getting a divorce!"

Tricia nodded sharply.

"I think you're in," she said, then scribbled some more and turned the notebook for the girls' inspection:

QUALIFICATIONS:

Must be a girl.
Must be in middle school.
Must have divorced parents.

"Uh-oh," Mei said as she read the list. "I don't qualify. My parents didn't get a divorce. My dad died."

"Hmmmm . . . ," Tricia said. "How did he die?" She wasn't sure why it mattered, but her role as leader was starting to feel as comfortable as a well-worn bathrobe.

"Cancer," Mei replied, making it sound more like a question.

Tricia nodded. "How long ago?"

"A long time. I was just a baby."

Tricia turned back to her notebook, erasing and scribbling.

"How's this: instead of 'must have divorced parents,' I wrote, 'must have stepparents.' "

Elizabeth's face sank. "Neither of my parents is remarried," she said glumly.

All heads turned to Tricia. "Okay, *here* are the qualifications," she said, scribbling some more. "Qualifications: Must be a girl. Must be in middle school. Must have a complicated family."

The girls contemplated the list for a minute, then nodded.

"That works," Hope said cheerfully. "But are you sure you can't think of some way to disqualify Leighton?" She glanced at Mei, who giggled.

"Why do you want to disqualify Leighton?" asked Tricia, who suddenly was taking all Right-Under matters very seriously.

"She won't even give us the time of day at school," Hope said. "She's A list. Mei and I are definitely B."

"Maybe even C," Mei said.

Hope nodded. "I can't believe she's even considering being in the same club with us. Trust me, if it wasn't for the math tutoring, she wouldn't consider breathing the same air as me."

"She probably won't come," Mei said.

"Anybody up there?"

The girls all jumped at the voice coming from below.

"Up here!" Tricia called, then leaned toward the girls. "She's got a golf cart," she said in a lowered voice. "I say she's in."

That logic won them over. The girls nodded as Leighton climbed the steps.

"I brought T-shirts!" she gushed as she lowered her head to walk through the door. "Every club needs T-shirts."

She started pulling the pink shirts from a bag and tossing them to the girls. Her lip curled when she saw Elizabeth. "Who are you?"

"This is Elizabeth," Tricia said protectively. "She's Hope's cousin. We just voted her in."

Leighton looked dubious. "Well . . . I don't have a T-shirt for her."

"That's okay," Elizabeth said quickly. "Maybe I can have one made after the meeting. They're so cute!"

Leighton, who was wearing her T-shirt, pushed out her already-developing chest to display her handiwork. The shirt was decorated with large letters: R.U.

"I used my mom's credit card to have them made. When my stepdad saw it, he said, 'R.U.?' and I was like, 'Am I what?' " She dissolved into giggles, then cast an annoyed glance at Elizabeth. "I guess I can try to have another shirt made."

Elizabeth smiled gratefully.

"Good," Tricia said, once again scribbling in her notebook. "She'll need one for the meetings. I've been jotting down some club rules."

She held them up for inspection:

CLUB RULES:

Meet every Thursday at 3 p.m. in the tree house.
Wear club T-shirt to meetings. (REQUIRED!!!)
Tell NO ONE what R.U. stands for.

The girls murmured their approval of the rules, and everyone but Elizabeth pulled their new shirts over what they were wearing. They giggled at the sudden plethora of pink, but Mei looked concerned.

"So we've got a place for the meetings . . . and we've got a time for the meetings . . . and we've got T-shirts for the meetings. But what will we *do* at the meetings?"

All eyes turned to Tricia. Uh-oh. Maybe she hadn't thought this through.

"Uh . . ." The girls' expressions were so expectant that she had to come up with something quick. Think . . . think . . .

Lists! Tricia loved lists.

"Here's what we'll do," she said. "We've all got hassles

associated with complicated families, right? For instance, I have a totally annoying half sister who gets all the attention in my family. And Mei's stepdad is the principal."

The girls' expressions were unanimous in sympathy.

"Hope has to put up with a stepmother," Tricia continued, "and Leighton's stepbrother is a geek."

"I like him," Mei said softly, but nobody noticed.

"And my parents are fighting for custody!" Elizabeth interjected cheerily.

"Exactly!" Tricia said. "We all have Right-Under problems. So here's what we'll do." She glanced at Hope, who was holding a thin stick she'd found on one of the tree house steps. Tricia took the stick from her and held it up.

"This is the Problem Stick," she said solemnly. "Each week, one of us will hold the Problem Stick. We'll take turns. The one holding the Problem Stick has to stand up and tell us about a Right-Under problem she's having. The rest of us will each write down a solution. Don't sign it, just write it anonymously. We'll read the solutions out loud and discuss which one we think is best. Then the person with the problem can report back to us about whether it worked."

She pulled out a marker, and wrote "Solutions" on the plastic bowl. As she set the bowl ceremoniously on the floor, the girls gazed, intrigued. Just an empty plastic bowl, but it had suddenly given shape and purpose to their club . . . maybe even to their summer. Was it really possible to pluck a solution out of a bowl?

"I dunno . . . ," Mei said in barely a whisper, giving voice to what everyone was thinking. "We can't expect a plastic bowl to change our lives."

"Maybe not," said Tricia. "But five heads are better than one. We all understand what the others are going through. What's the worst that can happen if we put our heads together and try to help each other?"

"What's the best that can happen?" Hope countered. "You guys can't make my dad unmarry my stepmother. We can't fire Mei's stepdad as principal. And we can't make your bratty little sister disappear."

Tricia blushed and lowered her head. Was that how she had characterized Everly? As a bratty little sister she wanted to make disappear? She felt ashamed. "I love my sister," she said softly. "I just hate always feeling second best . . . you know?"

The girls nodded, and Mei reached over and touched Tricia's arm. "We know," she said. "Like a leftover. We all feel that way. That's why we formed the Right-Under Club, remember?"

The tree house was silent except for the sound of birds chirping outside in the warm June sunshine.

"And it's not like any of our solutions will involve hiring a hit man," Leighton said, speaking her mind so brashly that the girls couldn't help laughing.

Tricia folded her hands and cleared her throat. "Okay, Right-Unders: It's time to put your problems in the Right-Unders' hands." She glanced at the notebooks and passed them out to the girls along with pencils. "Good thing I brought extras," she said as she handed one to Elizabeth. "And, hey: let's keep Right-Under journals during the summer."

Leighton's eyebrows arched. "Who are you, my English teacher?"

"So writing's not your thing?" Hope asked, rolling her eyes. "I'm shocked."

"It's bad enough my mom's making me study math," Leighton complained with a sniff. "I am not wasting my whole summer on schoolwork."

Tricia held up her hands in surrender. "Okay, okay," she said. "Journaling is optional. But be sure to bring your notebook to meetings. Let's put our club name on the cover. And our motto."

The girls' brows furrowed.

"Which means, of course, that we need a club motto," Tricia said with a grin.

The girls tapped their pencils against their notebooks as they thought. Hope's eyes brightened. "How's this: We R There for U."

It had a nice ring to it. The girls wrote it on their notebooks.

5

Tricia cleared her throat. It was time for serious business.

"Okay," she said somberly. "Let's decide who gets to hold the Problem Stick for this meeting."

The cedar beams squeaked as the girls self-consciously adjusted their positions on the floor. They cast their eyes downward, up at the ceiling, at the sunbeams peeking through slits in the wood—anywhere to avoid each other's gazes. Sure, they all had problems, but having to put them on display suddenly felt a little like going to school in your underwear. Would this really work? Would the girls be willing to bare their souls?

Hope wondered if the problem had to concern her complicated family. Frankly, she had a more pressing matter. Her biggest problem right now was her hair. Other girls could pull theirs back in a bouncy ponytail or a chic French braid, or just wash and go without worrying that their hair would set off in an entirely different direction. Why couldn't she exchange her red ringlets for sleek, straight hair like Mei's or Leighton's? Sure, Leighton was a snob, but there was no denying how beautiful she was. Why did Hope have to look just like her mother? She swallowed hard and tamped down the thought.

Mei was struggling, too. Her biggest problem right now was that she had a crush on Leighton's stepbrother, Kyle, who, like every other boy at Clearview Middle School, barely knew she existed. But she couldn't exactly disclose that to the group. She was so shy, she couldn't fathom a guy's even noticing her, let alone liking her. She was usually able to talk to her mother about her feelings, but with a new baby on the way, her mom was way too preoccupied with swollen ankles to even give lip service to Mei's concerns. Mei alternated between feeling invisible and sticking out like a sore thumb because of her Asian features—a distinct rarity in Clearview, and now even weird in her own house, thanks to a blue-eyed stepfather. She wished she looked like Leighton. . . .

Forget it, Leighton said to herself. The idea had popped into her head so spontaneously—Maybe I should come clean and tell my real problem—that she didn't have time to censor the thought. Of course she couldn't write that problem down. She was annoyed at herself for even considering it. She had a reputation to protect, after all. The most beautiful and popular girl at Clearview Middle School wasn't about to blow her cover.

Elizabeth tapped her pencil rhythmically against her knee. Her main problem was so overwhelming, she couldn't even wrap her brain around it. She had perfected the art of pushing it out of her mind. The only time it crept back in was at night, when she would scream out loud during a nightmare or amble through the house during a bout of anxious sleepwalking. So it didn't even occur to her to write *that* problem down.

Tricia, as usual, didn't have a moment's hesitation in coming up with her problem. It was so all-consuming that she thought about it at least a dozen times a day. She knew exactly what her problem was. What she didn't know was how the Right-Under Club might be able to help.

"Has everybody thought of a problem?" Tricia asked.

Hope knitted her brow and mouthed something at Mei. Mei shook her head quickly and looked away.

"What?" Tricia probed.

"Mei kinda has a problem that's coming up right away," Hope said.

"Hope!" Mei scolded.

"Well, that's what we're here for," Hope said. "Stop being so shy. We're all going to tell our problems. We might as well start with you since you need an immediate solution."

Mei looked hesitant, but as far as Tricia was concerned, the matter was settled. She handed the Problem Stick to Mei, who took it reluctantly.

"You have to stand when you tell your problem," Tricia said, and Mei slowly rose to her feet. She smoothed her pink T-shirt and cleared her throat.

"Um . . ."

"Louder, please," Tricia prompted.

"Um," Mei said more loudly, "my stepdad wants . . . well, he asked me . . . he kind of said he'd like . . ."

"Get to the point!" Hope said.

"He wants me to paint a mural in the school lunchroom," Mei blurted out, then exhaled nervously.

"You see, Mei's stepdad . . . ," Hope began to say, but Tricia shushed her.

"Mei has the Problem Stick," she reminded her. "Let her talk."

Mei cleared her throat again. "It doesn't seem like a big deal," she said.

Elizabeth shrugged. "Then what's the problem?" she asked, adjusting her glasses.

"See, Mei feels like—" Hope said in a rapid-fire tumble before the others shushed her again.

"Mei?" Tricia said.

"Hope makes a big deal about what a great artist I am," she said, wincing, "but I'm really not. And even if I was, I still wouldn't want to show anybody my work, let alone the whole school. I'm afraid the kids will make fun of me. And I feel like my stepdad's just using me for free labor."

The girls *mmmm*ed their understanding.

Mei offered a bashful smile. "That's my problem."

She handed the Problem Stick back to Tricia and sat on the floor of the tree house, leaning back on her hands and crossing her legs at the ankles.

"Okay, girls: our first problem," Tricia said, exhilarated that their club was taking shape. A real problem! This club was going to be great.

"Time to write a solution in your notebooks," she continued. When you're finished, tear out the paper, fold it twice and put it in the Solutions Bowl." She glanced at her watch. "Let's take five minutes to write down our solutions, then I'll read them out loud."

"Do I have to follow your advice?" Mei asked.

Again, everyone looked to Tricia for the answer. "We can't force you to do anything you don't want to do," she said reasonably. "But remember that your fellow Right-Unders have your best interests at heart. We'll read the solutions and discuss which one we like. Then you do what you think is best, weighing our advice very carefully. But you have to report back to us at next Thursday's meeting."

She glanced at her watch again. "Right-Unders: The time starts now."

As the girls concentrated, Hope began humming the *Jeopardy!* theme song.

"Do you mind?" Leighton snapped.

Hope rolled her eyes but piped down.

Silence fell as the girls turned in separate directions for privacy. Mei glanced anxiously from one notebook to the next.

"Can I have a potato chip?" Elizabeth asked softly.

"Shhh!" the others said in unison.

"Elizabeth, we need complete silence while we come up with our solutions," Tricia explained patiently.

Elizabeth blushed and returned to her notebook.

Tricia wrote and erased, wrote and erased, then wrote some more. This was serious business.

A few more minutes passed.

"Time's up," Tricia said after checking her watch.

The girls ripped pieces of paper from their notebooks, folded them twice and dropped them in the Solutions Bowl as Tricia passed it from one Right-Under to the next.

"Can we have chips while you read the solutions?" Elizabeth asked. Tricia tightened her lips but opened the potato-chip sack and passed it to Elizabeth.

"Okay, girls, here's the first solution," she said, picking a piece of paper from the bowl and unfolding it. "'SOLUTION: Sabbitoj! Do such an awfull job that your stepdad will never ask you to help him again.'"

Tricia couldn't help smiling. She hadn't known Leighton long, but the spelling—not to mention the sentiment—made her pretty sure who the author was.

"What was that first word?" Elizabeth asked.

"Sabotage," Tricia said. "It means to mess up a project on purpose. Should we discuss this solution or read the others first?"

"Read them all, then we can talk about which one we think is best," Hope said.

"Okay. Here are the other solutions." Tricia unfolded the papers and read them one by one:

"SOLUTION: Explain to your stepdad that you feel used and refuse to paint the mural.

"SOLUTION: Tell your mom how you feel and let her tell your stepdad that you won't do it.

"SOLUTION: Paint the best mural ever! Everybody at school will be talking about how talented you are."

Tricia paused after reading the final solution.

"I like the first one best," Leighton said after a few seconds.

Hope stifled a giggle.

"What are you laughing at?" Leighton spat.

"Sabotage is a stupid idea," Hope said coolly, tossing a curl over her shoulder. "The only person that will hurt is Mei. She's a great artist. People should know."

"Hmmm." Leighton sneered. "I wonder which solution was yours."

Hope turned toward Mei. "Go for greatness. Who cares why your stepdad is asking you to paint the mural? This is your chance to shine."

Elizabeth bounced in excitement. "That's an awesome solution, Hope."

Mei frowned. "The only person who thinks I'm great is you, Hope," she said. "And I appreciate it . . . but I'm not. I don't want to make a fool of myself. Besides, my stepdad will be expecting daisies and butterflies. That's not my style."

"Then show him your style!" Tricia said. "Show the world your style. I think Hope is right. This is your chance."

Mei hugged her knees against her chest. "I can usually talk to my mom about my problems, but she gets this panicky expression on her face when I complain about Stan. She's so desperate for us to get along, especially now that she's pregnant."

"I totally get that," Tricia concurred. "My mom has a smile practically pasted on her face when Troy and I are together, as if she can make us like each other just by sending out happy vibes. It's so fake . . . not like with my real dad, who's okay with whatever kind of mood I'm in."

"Ahem," Leighton said, raising an eyebrow. "I thought we were talking about Mei's problem."

"It's okay," Mei said. "Tricia's right. I don't remember what it's like to have a real dad, but I know what it's like to fake it with a stepdad." She laced her fingers together and squeezed. "Not that I'm always faking it. He's nice, and sometimes it's cool having him around. But if it's *not* cool, I always have to fake it for my mom's sake."

Tricia shook her head. "I don't fake it," she insisted. "I keep it real, and if Troy doesn't like it, that's his problem."

"And your mom's problem," Mei said.

"Too bad." Tricia sniffed. "I didn't ask her to marry him."

A warm breeze whistled softly through the cedar slats.

"Mom says we'll feel more like a family after the baby is born," Mei said.

Tricia opened her mouth to respond, then changed her mind.

Hope leaned closer to Mei. "Paint your mural," she said. "You really are talented."

"Is it unanimous, Right-Unders?" Tricia asked. She, Hope and Elizabeth raised their hands. Leighton hesitated, then extended a hand weakly in the air.

"Our advice: Paint the mural, paint it your way and show the world your true colors." Tricia smiled at her cleverness.

Mei bit her lower lip. "I don't know . . . ," she said. "I'll give it a try, I guess. For the Right-Unders."

"For the Right-Unders," Tricia repeated, holding the Problem Stick aloft ceremoniously. "Don't forget to report back to us next Thursday."

6

"Focus, Leighton."

Leighton pushed her sunglasses onto the tip of her nose and cut her eyes at Hope. She'd finally agreed to a tutoring session, but only if it was poolside. It was Saturday, after all.

Hope had gamely stuck a math book into a nylon bag, along with her beach towel and sunscreen, then made it to the neighborhood pool at two p.m. sharp, just as they'd agreed. But as soon as she opened the gate and scanned the pool area, she calculated that the chances of a productive afternoon were slim to none. There was Leighton, sprawled out on a lounge chair in a turquoise bikini and glistening with suntan lotion. Several boys buzzed around her like mosquitoes, laughing too loudly and gesturing too broadly. Occasionally, one would dive or do a cannonball into the sparkling blue pool, then spin his soaked head in Leighton's direction to see whether she'd noticed. Leighton mostly looked bored, and Hope doubted she'd find math much more interesting.

Of course, she was right. As Hope pulled up a chair beside Leighton's and droned on about factors and variables, Leighton applied lip gloss, smacked her lips together and tilted her head farther back for maximum sun exposure.

"If you don't focus, you'll never learn this stuff," Hope said.

"Hey, Leighton, watch this!" one of the boys called before doing a badly executed somersault into the pool that left him grimacing in pain as he smacked the water with his back.

Leighton sputtered giggles into her fingertips. "He is so immature," she concluded to no one in particular—certainly not to Hope, who seemed no more noteworthy than the lounge chair she was sitting in.

"Leighton!" Hope cried in frustration. "Are you listening to me or not?"

Leighton sat up straight and glared at Hope. "Like, a little louder, please," she said through clenched teeth. "My mom is sitting three chairs over and there's a chance, just a chance, she couldn't hear you."

"Why am I bothering if you won't pay attention?"

Leighton swatted her hand through the air as if Hope was a gnat. "I'm listening, I'm listening. Variables. Those are the Xs and Ys. See? Just keep talking. My mom's watching."

Hope gritted her teeth. How could she have agreed to be in a club with this . . . this . . . this princess? Leighton was beyond infuriating.

"Hope! Leighton!"

The girls glanced toward the gate. Tricia, Mei and Elizabeth closed it behind them and walked toward their friends.

Leighton sank deeper in her chair as they approached. "Do you have to scream my name across the pool?" she muttered, then cast a critical eye on Elizabeth. "You definitely need to start hanging out at the pool. If you were any whiter, I'd go blind looking at you. And what's with the swimsuit? Did you have to go to Baby Gap to find something with little flowers on it?"

Elizabeth blushed.

"Hi, girls!" another voice called from the gate. They looked over and saw Hope's stepmother, Jacie, walking in with Mei's mom, whose one-piece swimsuit bulged over her pregnant midriff.

Leighton blinked hard. "How could anybody go out in public like that?" she asked, looking Mei's mother up and down. "It should be against the law for moms to wear swimsuits anyhow."

"I think my mom looks great," Mei said quietly, but nobody noticed.

"Hey, Leighton, come play Marco Polo!" one of the boys called from the water. Leighton ignored him.

"He's talking to you," Tricia said.

"That doesn't mean I'm listening." Leighton adjusted her sunglasses and stretched her legs.

"He's so cute," Elizabeth said.

"Then you go play with him," Leighton snapped. "The boys in this neighborhood are so annoying. Besides, I'm not into boys. I'm into men. I'm crushing on a high school hottie named Scott." She giggled. "A hottie named Scottie. I can't wait till I'm in high school."

"If you don't pass math, you'll never make it," Hope said. "We're supposed to be studying."

Leighton wrinkled her nose. "How can I concentrate with all you people hovering around me? Besides, you're blocking my sun."

Hope narrowed her eyes and snapped the math book shut. "I

think Leighton's absorbed all the math today that her brain can handle. Lesson over." She looked mischievously at the other girls. "Last one in's a rotten egg."

She sprang to her feet, ran to the side of the pool and dove in. Tricia followed her with a hearty squeal; then Mei and Elizabeth jumped in.

"You're splashing me!" Leighton whined from her lounge chair.

"Aw," Hope whispered conspiratorially to the other girls as their heads bobbed from the water. "The princess is getting wet."

"We *told* you she was snotty," Mei said to Tricia.

"Off the charts," Tricia agreed.

"She's really beautiful, though," Elizabeth said, tugging self-consciously at her flowered swimsuit. "And she *is* a Right-Under."

"Well . . . ," Hope said, "that could be changed."

Mei's eyebrows arched in panic. "Hey, wait a minute! I spilled my guts at the last meeting. She knows all this . . . stuff about me. If we kick her out, she'll blab it to the whole world."

"All she knows is that your stepdad wants you to paint a mural," Hope countered.

"It's not just the mural," Mei said. "It's . . . I don't know. It feels really personal, you know?"

Tricia nodded. "Mei's right. We've already made Leighton a Right-Under. Let's just hang in there. It'll be cool."

The girls nodded reluctantly.

"Hey, speaking of the mural," Tricia said, "how's it going?"

"I start Monday," Mei said, still looking worried. "*If* I start. Are we sure this Right-Under Club is such a good idea?"

"Of course it is!" Elizabeth said more loudly than she intended. She lowered her reddened face. "I mean . . . I like clubs. Especially this one."

Hope smiled at her cousin. "Then I say it's settled. We R There for U. And even for Leighton, if you guys insist. Just don't say I didn't warn you."

Tricia's eyes gleamed. "Hey," she said, nodding in Leighton's direction. "It looks like the princess has fallen asleep. Who's up for giving her a wake-up call? Follow me."

The girls exchanged dubious expressions but giggled as they followed Tricia out of the pool and over to Leighton's lounge chair. Tricia mouthed directions to them, pointing for clarity, as Leighton snoozed.

They looked like they would burst with anticipation as Tricia started the countdown on her fingers. Five . . . four . . . three . . . two . . .

One.

Tricia and Hope quickly grabbed Leighton's arms as Mei and Elizabeth grabbed her legs.

"Wha . . . wha . . . *hey!*" Leighton yelped as they carried her potato-sack style to the side of the pool, then tossed her in.

They whooped triumphantly as Leighton floundered in the pool and groped for her sunglasses.

"Are you *insane?*" she shrieked.

The girls doubled over in laughter, and after a moment of sputtering indignation, even Leighton couldn't help grinning. "I will get even," she said, playfully splashing them, "when you least expect it."

"Yeah, well, in the meantime," Tricia responded cheerfully, "let's have fun!"

She did a cannonball into the water and the others followed one by one, creating a sparkling, chlorine-scented rain shower.

"You guys are so dead," Leighton said through her giggles.

"What happened to the math lesson?" her mom called from the side of the pool.

But the Right-Unders were laughing too hard to respond.

• • •

Elizabeth's Right-Under Journal

Saturday, June 12

Hi, Right-Under Journal. This is my first entry. I totally LUV this club. I feel like this will be the greatest summer of my whole life, even tho it started out 2 B the worst. Thank heaven I talked Mom into letting me stay with Hope until school starts back. I miss her and Dad, but I don't miss all the crying and yelling. True, Mom calls me on the phone like twice a day (and usually starts crying by the time we hang up), but I feel like I can have a real summer now. I wish she and Dad didn't hate each other, and I wish they'd quit making me feel like a blob of taffy, with each of them pulling from different ends. But I can't do anything about it. (NOT THAT I HAVEN'T TRIED!!!) So I'll have fun instead. I LUV my R.U. friends, even "the princess." (Inside joke!!!) We had so much fun at the pool today. Speaking of which . . . Hope and Jacie are taking me shopping tomorrow for new swimsuits! I'm getting them from the juniors department, even if I have to stuff tissues in the tops to make them fit. (lol.) Wish me luck! RIGHT-UNDERS ROCK!!!

7

"Mei! Five minutes!"

Stan's voice boomed from the bottom of the stairs. Mei winced. He was so loud. Couldn't her mother have anticipated what an awkward fit Stan would be in their family?

Mei placed a baseball cap over her dark, layered hair, then walked into her mother's bedroom.

"Hi, honey," her mom said, yawning and stretching her arms in her bed. "What time is it?"

"A little after eight. I'm going to school with Stan today, remember?"

"Oh, right." Her mother propped herself up on an elbow. "I forgot it was Monday. Are you ready to get started?"

Mei sat on the bed next to her mother. "Not really." She stared at her interlaced fingers. "I'm dreading this, Mom."

"Oh, honey, the baby's kicking!" Mei's mother took Mei's hand and placed it on her stomach. "This little guy is so much more active than you were."

Mei managed a smile. "Are you cooking today?" she asked. Her mom was a caterer, using their kitchen as a home base.

"Just a birthday cake," her mother replied. "But it'll be a

pain. The birthday girl's present is a cruise, and the cake is supposed to look like a cruise ship, complete with little cabin windows and swimming pools on the deck. Maybe I'll give the teeny little passengers nasty sunburns, just for fun."

Mei laughed. Her mom was so artistic, but the only time her talent really shone was when clients let her follow her best instincts instead of micromanaging. Most people, Mei was learning, were micromanagers.

Mei's mom squeezed her hand and said, "I wish you were going to be home to help me."

"Now, that could be arranged."

"*Mei!*"

Stan was bellowing again from the bottom of the stairs, making both of them jump. "You better go," Mei's mother said, winking at her.

"Right." Mei leaned over and kissed her mother's cheek. "Bon voyage."

Mei straightened her baseball cap and trotted down the stairs.

"Mei, principals don't get a summer vacation, you know," Stan said testily. "You'll have to pick up the pace if you want me to let you paint that mural. I have to be at the office every morning by eight-thirty sharp."

Mei's jaw dropped. "If I want you to let me?"

But Stan was already jangling his car keys and ushering her toward the door. "Let's go, let's go!"

Mei rolled her eyes and walked with him to the driveway. She cringed getting into his car, which was plastered with tacky Clearview Middle School bumper stickers. Did he have to make sure the whole world knew he was the principal?

Stan fiddled with the radio station for a few seconds as they drove down the street, then turned it off. "So!" he said, making Mei jump. "Tell me what you have in mind for that mural."

I don't have anything in mind. It was your idea, Mei thought, but her only response was a shrug.

"Remember, we're the Clearview Comets. Think school spirit. Think fun!"

"I don't think you and I really have the same taste," Mei said, but in such a small voice that Stan didn't hear her. He was forever asking her to repeat herself, or worse, ignoring her altogether. So annoying.

Now that Stan had finished barking his ideas, he was quiet for the rest of the trip, turning the radio back on and whistling to a song. He spotted a couple of familiar faces on the ride and waved so heartily that Mei thought his hand might fly off. By the time they arrived at school, she had sunk so low in her seat that she could barely see out the window.

"Time to get started!" Stan said, and she followed him into the school. She had to scurry to keep up with him; he took huge strides with his long gangly legs. He reminded Mei of a goose.

Once they were inside the building, Stan opened the door to the office suite, where two secretaries sat at desks.

"Ladies!" he greeted them. "You remember my beautiful stepdaughter, Mei, don't you? Mei? Ms. Winston, Ms. Pollard."

The office ladies smiled and nodded. Mei smiled back.

"Mei's going to paint our cafeteria mural!" Stan boomed. The office ladies oohed. Mei wished the floor would open up and swallow her whole.

"We've all got a lot of work to do today," Stan said. "Mei, I believe all your supplies are set up in the cafeteria. So . . . let's get started!"

He opened the door and sent her on her way with a sweep of his arm. Mei was relieved that he was staying put in his office. At least she would have some privacy. She walked into the cafeteria, surveying the paint cans, brushes, pans, rollers and swaths of broadcloth spread under the wall she was painting. She put her hands on her hips and sighed. "Might as well get this over with. . . ."

What would she paint? Hmmm . . . Clearview: Nothing subtle about that image, but she couldn't stomach the idea of rolling pastures, puffy clouds and baby blue skies. Yechhh. She thought harder. Comets: Now, that image had potential. Her mind clicked off the possibilities. Yes, comets . . . she could make this work.

The first thing she needed was the background of a rich night sky. She dipped the thickest brush into the darkest paint.

As she slapped the strokes against the wall, she found herself swaying to a lazy cadence playing in her head. Her thoughts turned dreamy and her expression softened. Her arm swung effortlessly. She was in the zone . . . her favorite place to be. The zone was when her art and her self merged. When she painted something she liked, she felt in retrospect that she hadn't created it; she'd merely discovered it in the universe and plucked it from the heavens. She wanted her comet wall to be filled with those wonders of the universe. *Swish, swish, swish* went the large brush. Dab, dab, dab went the smaller one. Stark blacks. Lush browns. Deep purples. Muted navy blues. The velvety cloak of night would provide the perfect backdrop for her universe of treasures.

Hours passed. Mei was on a roll and didn't stop for a second, not even for a snack. She lost all track of time in the zone. Her night sky had lulled her into total serenity. Why had she dreaded this wonderful project? Why hadn't she jumped at the chance for free supplies and the blank canvas of an entire wall? What a great experience this was turning out to be. . . .

"*Mei!*"

Mei's arm jerked at the sound of the voice, leaving a jagged slash of paint on the wall.

"Stan . . . ," she replied, turning to face him. It was the first human contact she'd had all morning. Or was it afternoon? As her stomach growled, she realized that it was probably past lunchtime.

"Mei!" Stan repeated, rushing to her side with long strides and swinging arms.

"What?" she asked, genuinely confused.

"What is this?" Stan sputtered, tossing an arm in the direction of her artwork.

"My mural," Mei responded, feeling a thud in her heart that marked her abrupt descent from the zone.

Stan shook his head, grasping for words. "This is school spirit? This is fun?"

Not anymore, Mei thought glumly.

"I'm not finished," she said in barely a whisper.

"I think maybe you are!" Stan said. "This is nothing but . . . gloppy dark colors! It's a mess. A dark, gloomy mess." He pursed his lips. "This is not what I had in mind, young lady."

"Fine," Mei said, her eyes filling with tears. "I just want to go home."

• • •

The ride home was silent. Stan tapped his fingers nervously on the steering wheel as Mei stared out her window, her chin quivering. He occasionally opened his mouth to speak, but then thought better of it. Mei was glad he was silent. She didn't want to talk to him. Ever.

When Stan pulled into the driveway, Mei swung her door open as soon as the car stopped, then ran ahead of him into the house.

"You home, honey?" her mom called from the kitchen, but Mei went straight up the stairs without responding. By the time Stan was in the door, her mom was at the foot of the stairs, craning her neck in search of her daughter.

Mei slammed her bedroom door, fell onto her bed and buried her face in her pillow, crying so hard that her stomach ached. She heard Stan talking to her mother downstairs but didn't register, didn't care, what he said.

As furious as she was at Stan, she was even angrier at herself. Why had she believed this would go any differently? She and Stan had never had anything in common, from their ethnicity to their stature to their personality. "A dark, gloomy mess." That was what he'd called her artwork. That was what she called her life.

What would she tell the Right-Unders? They meant well, but Mei couldn't help feeling a little betrayed. What did they know about anything? Who were they to tell her how to solve her problems? She'd probably quit the club. She was even mad at Hope for giving her confidence in her talent. She was no artist. She was a joke.

Tap, tap, tap.

Someone was knocking on her door. Her mom, no doubt. Stan's knock was loud enough to shake the shutters off the windows.

"Go away, please," Mei called.

But the door creaked open. Her mom walked in and came over to her bed.

"Honey?"

Mei buried her face deeper in her pillow.

"Honey, I want you to sit up and look at me."

Her mother's voice was kind but firm. Mei roughly rubbed her face against the pillow to dry her tears, then sat up.

"Stan told me what happened," her mom said, sitting on the edge of her bed. "Mei, I'm so sorry."

Mei put her face in her hands, but her mother pulled them away.

"Look at me, Mei. Stan was wrong," she said indignantly. "He had no right asking you to do him a favor, then judging you so harshly. And he had no right to condemn your artwork when you were just getting started."

Stan appeared at the doorway. "I didn't mean to hurt your feelings, Mei," he said. "It's just . . . all that black. I wanted something bright and cheery."

Mei's mother cleared her throat sharply and shot Stan a withering look. "Close the door, please," she said. "I'm having a private conversation with my daughter."

Stan did as he was told. Mei felt an urge to hug her mother, but she was still too hurt. It felt so good to have her mother's support, her undivided attention.

"If he wants bright and cheery, he can hang rainbow posters in the cafeteria," her mother said, making Mei giggle in spite of herself. "If he wants art, he came to the right person." She took Mei's hands. "You're a wonderful artist. And you're going to finish that mural."

Mei shook her head vigorously. "No way. I'm never painting again."

Her mother raised an eyebrow. "Very dramatic," she said. "But your talent won't let you shake it loose. Even if you use it to paint tiny swimming pools on birthday cakes, it'll find a way to express itself. Creativity's like a bad penny. It keeps turning up."

"Maybe so . . . but I'll never do anything for him again."

Her mother sighed. "Then don't do it for him. Do it for me. Better yet, do it for you. Trust your instincts and finish that mural just the way you planned. Stan promised me he won't go into the cafeteria until you're finished. Then, if he doesn't like it, he can paint over it."

Mei rolled her eyes. "Yippee," she said. "I'll spend a week of my summer totally wasting my time."

Her mom shook her head. "You'll spend a week of your summer expressing yourself. There's no better use of your time, honey."

Mei still wasn't entirely convinced, but she knew she'd be back in that cafeteria at eight-thirty sharp the next morning. She'd do it for her mom. She'd do anything for her mom.

• • •

HoPeLess has just signed on.

HoPeLess: mei-day, mei-day! how did it go at skool 2day? did you have fun painting?

artsyMEI: it was almost as fun as the time i wrecked my bike and knocked out my 2 front teeth.

HoPeLess: y? what happened?

artsyMEI: long story . . . let's just say my stepdad is NOT my biggest fan. my mural isn't exactly blowing him away.

HoPeLess: What did u paint?

artsyMEI: i'm not finished yet, but my masterpiece is a mess-terpiece as far as stan is concerned. lol

HoPeLess: what does he know?

artsyMEI: he knows he hates it. but mom is making me finish it anyway.

HoPeLess: it'll be ok! just trust your instincts.

artsyMEI: my instincts told me I never should have done this in the 1st place!

HoPeLess: hang in there. and remember: we R there for U.

artsyMEI: thanks. what did u do 2day?

HoPeLess: went swimming with elizabeth. poor kid. her parents are stressing her out with all their fighting. every time she gets off the phone with her mom, she practically breaks out in hives. but she just got 2 new swimsuits, so she's in a good mood.

artsyMEI: i could have pinched leighton's head off when she made fun of her flowered swimsuit. i thought it was really pretty.

HoPeLess: i told elizabeth not to listen to Leighton, but i know how hard it is to tune that girl out.

artsyMEI: my mom's banging on my door telling

me 2 go 2 bed. i gotta get back to my mess-terpiece 1st thing in the a.m.
HoPeLess: Good luck! I know u can do it.
artsyMEI has signed off.
HoPeLess has signed off.

8

"The second official meeting of the Right-Under Club will now come to order."

Tricia tapped the Problem Stick against the cedar wall of the tree house.

"Leighton's not here yet," Mei pointed out.

"Oooh, there's a big problem," Hope said. The girls giggled just as they heard Leighton's footsteps padding up the tree house steps. As she crouched to walk in the door, they abruptly fell silent and averted their eyes.

She glanced around the room, then tossed the T-shirt she was holding to Elizabeth.

"Your shirt," she said.

Elizabeth beamed. "Thank you!" She pulled her pink R.U. shirt over the one she was wearing. "Oh . . . and I got two new swimsuits at the mall last weekend." She searched Leighton's face for a sign of approval.

"Throw me in the pool again and you're dead," Leighton muttered.

Elizabeth's face brightened. "You looked so funny when we threw you in," she said, bouncing on her legs.

"Remember, I'll get even. When you least expect it." But even Leighton was smiling at the memory.

"Whatever," Tricia said playfully. "Let's begin our second official Right-Under Club meeting."

She opened her spiral-bound notebook and poised her pencil. "Let's start with old business. Last week, we heard Mei's problem—having to paint a mural in the school cafeteria for her stepdad—and our advice was to paint the greatest mural ever. How did it go, Mei?"

Mei stared down at her folded hands. "Well . . ."

"Louder, please!" Elizabeth said, even though Hope had already given her the 411 on Mei's week. The T-shirt made her feel so . . . official.

Mei looked at Hope, who gave her a reassuring nod. "I took your advice," Mei said. "And it was a disaster."

The girls leaned in.

"Well . . . it started out as a disaster," Mei continued. "I started the mural on Monday, and when Stan came to check out my work later in the day, he freaked. I'd just gotten started; I was painting a dark sky for a background, and that's the only part I'd finished. Anyhow, all he saw was . . . let's see, how did he put it? . . . 'a dark, gloomy mess.' "

She frowned at the memory, lowering her eyes. Tricia frowned in indignation, but Leighton murmured, "Black *is* pretty gloomy." Hope shushed her, and all eyes turned back to Mei.

"He wanted to just paint over the whole thing . . . my vision wasn't 'cheery and fun' . . . but my mom insisted that he let me finish. Not that I wanted to. She told Stan he couldn't see it until I was done."

"So?" Tricia said. "How'd he like it?"

"I'm not finished yet," Mei said. "I'll finish it tomorrow."

"How does it look?" Tricia asked.

Mei smiled faintly for the first time since the meeting had started. "I like it," she acknowledged, and the girls smiled back. "I figured since Stan already hated it and would probably paint over it anyway, why not really go for it and follow my instincts?"

Hope placed her hand on Mei's shoulder. "I can't wait to see it."

"It's nothing special," Mei quickly qualified. "But . . . I don't know . . . I guess it's okay."

"I bet it's great," Hope said. "And who cares what your stepdad thinks? His idea of great art is probably a clown painting. 'Cheery and fun.' "

The girls laughed.

"I draw clowns really well," Leighton said, and Hope groaned.

Tricia tapped the Problem Stick impatiently on the floor. "Mei followed our advice, and now I think it's our job to support her," she said. "We should be there tomorrow when she shows the mural to her stepdad."

Mei winced. "Thanks, but I get nervous when anybody sees my stuff. No audience, please."

"Mei, the whole school's going to see your 'stuff' every day at lunch from now on," Hope said reasonably. "The point of art is to share your talent with the world. It's time to start sharing."

"I'm sure he'll paint over it," Mei muttered.

"In that case, we should see it while it's still there," said Leighton.

"Either way, we're going to see it," Tricia said. "What time should we be at the school tomorrow?"

Mei sighed in resignation. "Three o'clock?"

"We'll be there," Tricia said. "Hey! It'll be my first time seeing my new school."

"Leighton, can we bum a ride on your golf cart?" Hope asked. "We can take the trail through the woods."

"Oooh, shotgun!" Elizabeth gushed, but was quickly silenced by the girls' disapproving expressions.

Leighton rolled her eyes. "I guess I can drive."

"We'll meet at two-forty-five by the guardhouse at the entrance of the subdivision," Tricia said.

"Remember, you guys, I'm not that talented, despite what Hope says," Mei said nervously. "I guess I can't stop you from coming, but you've got to be honest with me. I don't want anybody's sympathy vote. If you don't like it, it's okay to say so."

"Oh, trust me, we will," Leighton said coolly.

"Right," Tricia agreed. "We owe it to each other as Right-Unders to be honest." She held the Problem Stick aloft. "I guess it's time for the next problem."

Hope reached for the stick. "Sorry to seem pushy," she said, "but can this be the week for my problem? It's kind of an emergency."

"Sure," Tricia said, and handed her the stick.

Hope grasped it tightly in both hands and rose to her feet. "Saturday's my birthday," she explained. "June nineteenth."

"Oh, right," Mei said quickly, embarrassed that she'd forgotten.

"The problem is my stepmother," Hope continued. "Jacie is . . . she's . . . well, she's nothing like me."

Mei nodded in confirmation.

"What's she like?" Tricia asked.

Hope wrinkled her nose as if a bad odor had wafted into the room. "She's a total fake. She loves anything showy—jewelry, expensive clothes, her country club membership . . . did I mention jewelry? . . . all the stuff I hate."

"What's wrong with jewelry?" Leighton said, but Hope ignored her.

"Jacie has been trying to transform me since she married my dad three years ago."

"Gotta give her props for trying," Leighton said under her breath.

"I have no interest in being some cookie-cutter Barbie," Hope said, ignoring Leighton's ensuing snicker, "but Jacie apparently can't catch a clue."

"Aunt Jacie's not that bad," Elizabeth said quietly.

"The problem," Hope said, "is that Jacie wants to treat me to a spa day for my birthday."

"Oooh!" Leighton twittered.

"We're supposed to get up early Saturday morning and get facials, pedicures, manicures, massages, haircuts, makeup . . . the whole bit."

"I'll go if you don't want to!" Leighton said, raising her hand.

"I don't want to," Hope said bitterly. "Jacie knows I hate that stuff, but she tries to force it down my throat anyway. I think she's mortified to have such a hideous stepdaughter."

"You're not hideous," Mei said.

"You're really not," Tricia agreed. "You've got the prettiest blue eyes. And I love your hair."

Leighton made a face.

"My hair's awful," Hope moaned. "I wish I had hair like . . ."

She stopped herself. No need to make Leighton's head any bigger than it already was.

"Like whose?" Leighton persisted.

"Like anybody's other than mine. It's totally thick, frizzy, unmanageable . . . just a mess."

"It's not a mess," Tricia insisted. "It's gorgeous. Truly."

Hope smiled weakly. "Regardless," she said, "a spa day with Jacie is my idea of torture. And on my birthday." She paused, sat down and handed the Problem Stick back to Tricia. "That's my problem."

Tricia nodded sharply. "Right-Unders, you know what to do next. Does everybody have their notebooks and pencils?"

The girls nodded, and Tricia glanced at her watch. "Then it's time to start writing. Your five minutes starts . . . now."

Once again, the girls adjusted their positions for privacy. Hope squirmed uncomfortably. She felt suddenly vulnerable, drawing attention to the part of herself she was usually trying her best to keep people from noticing: her looks. Hair too red, skin too pale, figure too lumpy . . . It was one thing to fill her own head with those thoughts; it was another to broadcast them to a whole group of girls, especially a group that included Leighton. Would she blab Hope's insecurities all over town? The tree house had a way of giving a false sense of security. Right outside was a tough, cruel world. Hope was mad at herself for baring her soul. Oh, well . . . too late.

"Time's up," Tricia said abruptly. "Time to put your solutions in the Solution Bowl."

She passed the plastic bowl around as one girl after another folded her solution twice, then dropped it in the bowl.

"Time for me to read them," Tricia said when the bowl was full.

"Why do you always get to read the solutions?" Leighton asked.

"Because she's the president," Elizabeth said protectively.

"Big whoop," Leighton said. "Hand the bowl over. I'm reading them this time."

She grabbed the bowl, flipped a lock of thick hair and sent it cascading over her shoulder. With an eyebrow raised ever so subtly, she read the solutions one by one:

"SOLUTION: Go and have fun! I don't think your stepmother is trying to remake you; she's just trying to have a good time with you.

"SOLUTION: Go! ! ! ! You need all the help you can get.

"SOLUTION: Go, but make sure the makeover suits your taste. This will give you a chance to show Jacie who you really are.

"SOLUTION: Pretend you have a stomachache and stay home."

The girls exchanged furtive glances. As they were getting to know each other better, it was tempting to guess who had written what. Only Leighton's solution required no guessing. Everybody was sure which one was hers.

"What do you think, girls? Which solution is best?" Tricia asked, a little annoyed at Leighton for wresting away her position of authority. She didn't much trust Leighton, either.

"Well," Mei said, "we're almost unanimous in our opinion that Hope should go. So that part of the solution seems settled."

"Settled for everybody but me!" Hope protested. "I like the stomachache idea."

Elizabeth grinned broadly.

"Hope, whether you have a spa day on your birthday or not, it sounds like you need to deal with this issue sooner or later," Tricia said. "If you feel like your stepmother is really trying to squeeze you into some mold, it's time to stand your ground."

"It's not that Jacie tries to mold her," Mei said. "She just tries to be helpful. Very helpful. I don't think she means any harm."

Hope frowned. "You don't know what it's like," she said. "She makes me feel hopeless."

To everyone's surprise, including Hope's, her eyes filled with tears. Mei reached over and squeezed her hand. "You're not hopeless," she said in barely a whisper. "You're beautiful."

Leighton sighed in exasperation. "Here's the deal," she said. "This is no biggie. In the first place, you should be thrilled about a spa day, and in the second, even if you aren't thrilled about it, what's the worst that could happen?"

The girls were silent as they shared the startling thought that Leighton had actually just made a lot of sense.

"That is a good point," Tricia said. "Who cares why your stepmother wants you to have a makeover? And who cares whether you like it or not? It's just one day."

Hope brightened slightly. "Yeah . . . it's just one day."

"You might even have fun!" Elizabeth said.

"Why don't you go along, too?" Tricia asked Elizabeth. "You know . . . moral support."

"Can't," Elizabeth replied. "My dad is coming to visit that day."

"Her dad is definitely not the spa type," Hope teased. "And let's face it: neither am I. But I'll go. And I like the advice about making sure the makeover suits my taste."

Tricia smiled proudly.

"Of course, I'm not exactly sure what my taste is," Hope continued, "but maybe this will be a chance for both Jacie and me to find out."

The girls nodded their approval.

Hope's eyes softened. "Spa day—ready or not, here I come."

9

Mei dabbed her final specks of paint on the wall, wiped her forehead with the back of her hand, then stood back to get a better look. She glanced at the clock on the adjoining wall: 2:56.

"Oh, gosh . . . ," she moaned aloud, suddenly filled with anxiety. The girls would be here any minute. It was time to unveil her mural. Why had she agreed to let them come? It was bad enough to imagine Stan seeing it for the first time. It was a terrible idea for the Right-Unders to be here when he saw it. Stan was sure to hate it—he'd made that clear enough—and there was no telling what he would say to embarrass her. And to have to worry about her friends' assessment of her artwork on top of all that? Bad idea. "Oh, gosh . . . ," she repeated.

Still, she couldn't help being just a little pleased. Even if everybody hated her mural, the fact was that she . . . well, she couldn't quite bring herself to say that she liked it, but she didn't hate it. And locking herself into this cafeteria every day for the past week had been . . . she sighed . . . it had been terrific. Particularly after the first day, when her mom had encouraged her to go for it, she had never felt such a flood of creativity. With every stroke of a brush, with every whiff of the paint, she felt she was doing what she had been born to do. Other people might not like her art, but she liked creating it. If nothing else, this week had made her absolutely sure of that.

Tap, tap, tap.

Mei sucked in her breath. They were here. No more hiding her art. It was time to lift the veil.

Her heart pounded so hard as she walked over to the cafeteria door that she thought it might burst out of her chest. She couldn't help giggling at the thought: "Girl paints mural, dies of heart attack," the headline would read. It would serve Stan right. She put her hand on the doorknob, inhaled deeply, then opened the door. There stood Stan, with the two office ladies and the Right-Unders hovering behind him.

"Come on in," she said.

As they walked in, one after the other, their eyes locked on the facing wall: Mei's mural. The first few moments were silent. Everyone's eyes narrowed, then squinted, then relaxed again. Then, almost all at once, their jaws dropped. Hope was the first to speak.

"Mei . . ." was all she could say.

Then, more silence. They were so intensely focused on the mural that Mei couldn't help staring at it, too. I really do like it, she thought.

As her project had progressed, the background of a velvety night sky had surrendered to a myriad of colors. Mei was fascinated by what stars might look like close up, and she had captured the image in intense fireballs of crimson, gold and mango. The stars seemed three-dimensional, as if stepping too close might suck the onlooker into the vortex of the bright infernos. The stars were the most dramatic aspects of the mural, but other elements were mesmerizing as well. There were the graceful arcs of asteroids . . . the coarsely textured blues and greens of planets . . . bright bursts of constellations, all with flecks of color that made it look as if the night sky was showering Earth with its treasures. On the right end of the mural, Mei had painted "Clearview Comets: Ablaze with Potential."

Mei stood taller. "What do you think?"

No one spoke right away, but that was okay. Mei's nervousness had already melted away. It didn't really matter now what anybody else thought.

"Mei," Hope whispered. "It's awesome."

The others nodded vigorously, as if the comment had unfrozen their heads.

"Awesome? It's . . . unbelievable," one of the office ladies said. "I just . . . can't believe it."

Mei smiled.

"Mei," Stan said quietly, "I had no idea you were this talented." He hugged her so spontaneously that Mei didn't have a chance to shrink from his embrace. And she didn't particularly want to.

"Thanks," she said.

Then Tricia started clapping . . . a slow, hard clap. Elizabeth joined her, then Hope, then Leighton, then . . . everyone was clapping. Clapping for Mei. Clapping for her night sky, ablaze with potential. Mei winked at the Right-Unders. She was glad they were here to share the moment.

• • •

"I brought you your birthday present early."

Hope held her front door open and Mei walked in, handing her the wrapped package. "It's nothing much."

"You didn't have to get me a present," Hope said, leading Mei into her bedroom.

Mei plopped onto the bed. "Well, in that case," she teased, reaching back for the present, but Hope laughed and held it out of reach.

Hope ripped into the paper. Jacie would have disapproved; she always slid a manicured fingernail delicately beneath the tape so she could leave the paper undamaged and recyclable. Hmmph. Hope flung the ripped paper on the floor and opened the rectangular box.

"Oh, Mei . . ." It was a miniature painting of Mei's mural . . . the stars, the asteroids, the planets.

"Besides my mom, you're the only one who's always encouraged my art," Mei said. "This is my way of saying thanks."

Hope sat on the bed beside Mei and gave her a hug. "It's weird," she said, carefully placing the painting on her bedside table. "I'm really having fun with the Right-Under Club, but . . . I'm kind of jealous sharing you with the other girls."

Mei nodded. "For so long, it's been just the two of us."

"Can you believe we're actually hanging out with Leighton Lockwood?" Hope whispered, sparking a round of sputtered laughter.

"Wait till school starts," Mei said. "She'll go right back to dissing us."

"But by then, we'll know all her secrets."

They laughed more, but nervously. As snobby as Leighton

was, their conversation was starting to feel vaguely like a betrayal. Mei decided to change the subject.

"Where's Elizabeth?"

"Out with Jacie, shopping for my birthday presents, I think," Hope said.

"I thought the spa day was your present."

Hope rolled her eyes. "Jacie goes overboard with everything. She'll probably have fifty presents for me to open."

"And that's a bad thing?"

"It's a Jacie thing."

"How long is Elizabeth staying?" Mei asked.

Hope shrugged. "I think everybody's playing it by ear. She needs a break from being in the middle of her parents' tug-of-war."

"Poor Elizabeth," Mei said.

"Yeah . . . I know she's just a little kid, but she loves being a member of the Right-Under Club. Thanks for putting up with her."

"I like her," Mei said. "And I like Tricia. And . . . I don't know . . . I'm even starting to tolerate Leighton."

They laughed some more, but Hope knew what she meant. The girls were starting to feel like more than fellow club members. They were starting to feel like friends.

10

Hope sat straight up in her bed and glanced at the clock on her bedside table. It was seven-forty-five.

The mail was never here that early, but there was always a chance. . . .

She hopped out of bed, pulled her red ringlets into an unruly ponytail, put on some shorts and a T-shirt, brushed her teeth, then sprang for the front door.

"There's the birthday girl!"

Uh-oh.

"Hi, Jacie," Hope said, pausing by the door as Jacie walked over and kissed her cheek.

"Happy birthday, sweetie! It's about time you got up. Our spa day starts in exactly"—she checked her watch—"one hour and fifteen minutes."

Hope twirled her finger in the air. Whoopee.

"Don't put on any makeup or fix your hair," Jacie said. "Remember, we're leaving that to the professionals today."

Hope resisted the urge to feign sticking her finger down her throat.

"Where are you going now?" Jacie asked.

"To check the mail," Hope said, trying to sound casual.

"At this time of day? You know the mail isn't here yet."

Hope blushed. "It's no biggie," she sniffed. "I just thought I'd check."

Jacie paused for a moment, then nodded. "You never know. The mailman might be early today. Can't hurt to check."

Hope flung the door open and trotted down the driveway to the mailbox at the edge of the yard. Her heart fluttered with excitement as she opened the mailbox door.

Nothing.

What was she thinking? Of course it was empty. It would probably be empty even after the mailman came.

She walked back in the door, where her dad greeted her.

"The birthday girl!" he said cheerily.

"Very original," Hope muttered, but she smiled at him.

"Ready for your spa day?" he asked.

"Of course she is," Jacie responded. "Every girl loves to be pampered. Hope, go ahead and eat some breakfast so we can get started. Time to get beautiful!"

Grrrrr . . .

"What time is Uncle Rob supposed to be here?" Hope asked her dad.

"Later this morning," he responded. "We're going to take Elizabeth to lunch, then maybe catch a movie."

Hope's heart sank. She wanted to catch a movie, too. The way she and her dad used to do. Just the two of them. Before Jacie.

"Don't see anything good," she whined.

"Oh, right," her dad responded. "We're going to see a *bad* movie. I should have made that clear." He tousled her hair and headed up the stairs to take a shower.

“I can’t believe you’re thirteen. A teenager!” Jacie gushed, leading Hope into the kitchen. “I was thirteen when I went to my first dance. I still remember the dress. Yellow taffeta.”

Gag. “I don’t think I’ll be going to any dances,” Hope said as Jacie broke eggs into a bowl and started scrambling them.

“Sure you will, honey,” Jacie responded. “That’s part of being a teenager.”

“Jacie, I don’t think my life as a teenager will have much in common with your life as a teenager.”

“Why do you say that?” Jacie asked, pouring the eggs into a skillet and heating them over the stove.

“Because you’re pretty. You were the kind of girl who got asked out to dances. I’m not.”

Hope wasn’t feeling sorry for herself . . . she was simply stating a fact.

Jacie tightened her bathrobe sash and walked over to the table, pulling up a seat next to Hope’s. “Hope, you so underestimate yourself,” she said, staring at her intently. “You always have.”

Always? What did Jacie know about always? Hope had already been nine when she’d gotten dragged into Jacie’s Junior League life.

“You are beautiful,” Jacie said. “That’s why I’m so excited about this spa day. You’ll learn from experts how to bring your beauty out.”

That made absolutely no sense. “If they have to *make* me beautiful, that means I’m not beautiful now,” Hope pointed out reasonably.

“You are,” Jacie insisted. “But you don’t know it yet. When you know it, so will everybody else.”

Hope felt like screaming in frustration. Why did Jacie always talk in circles?

Jacie walked back to the stove. "Sometimes all it takes," she said, pulling the pan from the stove, "is just that extra bit of effort."

Now, that advice Hope could relate to. She needed that extra bit of effort to refrain from scrambling some eggs over Jacie's head.

• • •

"How ya doin'?"

What kind of question was that?

"I'm lying here with sticky goop on my face and cucumber slices on my eyes," Hope responded. "Doesn't get much better than that."

Jacie laughed in her irritating high-pitched trill. "Isn't she a riot?" she said to the spa ladies.

The only good news about having cucumbers on her eyes, in Hope's estimation, was that it signaled the halfway mark of her spa day. She had already endured a pedicure and manicure. The only things left after the facial were a massage, a haircut and a makeup session.

The first half of the day might have been tolerable if Jacie hadn't asked her every five minutes, "How ya doin'?"

You tell me, she felt like responding. How am I doing? Am I passing your little test?

But she was trying to go easy on the sarcasm. Her dad had pulled her aside before they left and begged her to be nice to Jacie. Jacie, he told Hope, wanted this day to be special.

Not much chance of that, unless the spa ladies could somehow transform her into a thin, leggy blonde like Jacie. Deep down, she wondered if her stepmother was setting her up to fail, so she could demonstrate to the world that despite her best efforts, Hope was officially hopeless.

The thought didn't make for a very relaxing massage, which was the next step. It seemed that the more the masseur dug his hands into Hope's shoulders, the tenser she became.

"Loosen up!" he told her periodically, at which point Jacie would lift her head from her own massage table and cast a disappointed look at Hope. As the day progressed, Hope became more of a disappointment.

At least they were almost done. After the massages, Hope and Jacie sat next to each other in swivel chairs in front of mirrors. Time for the most excruciating part: the makeover.

It began with a hairdresser combing through Hope's unruly curls and frowning. "You've got a lot of hair," she said, an observation Hope heard every time she got her hair cut. Never once had she mistaken it for a compliment.

"Isn't it beautiful?" Jacie cooed from her seat, where a hairdresser was happily snipping away at her fine, straight locks. "If only my hair had that body."

That was another one Hope heard a lot: her hair had "body." People with sleek hair always feigned dismay at their lack of "body." Hope wanted to hurl.

The hairdresser cut a couple of inches from Hope's hair, at which point it looked . . . exactly as bushy as it had before. "The only hope is to shave it," Hope told her.

"Positive!" Jacie scolded. "We're being positive today!"

Grrrrr . . .

The makeup artist didn't frown quite as much as the hairdresser, but Hope sensed her disapproval.

"You've got to clean your face very thoroughly every night before you go to bed," she said sternly, making it clear that Hope had not. Still, Hope admired her handiwork. As the blush, eye shadow, mascara and lipstick were smoothed, brushed and spread onto her face one by one, Hope couldn't help noticing her features. Yes, her cheekbones really were prominent, and yes, her bright blue eyes did sparkle. And everyone commented on her peaches-and-cream complexion. If only she wasn't so pale . . .

"All done," the makeup artist said.

"See how pretty?" Jacie cooed. "Now, if only Hope would just keep it up."

The makeup artist smiled, but Hope seethed.

"Can we take you home so you can pretty her up every morning?" Jacie asked the makeup artist with a laugh.

Okay, that was the last straw. Hope's eyes burned with hot tears, and she rushed out to the car as Jacie paid the bill.

By the time Jacie joined her in the car, tears were streaming down Hope's cheeks.

"What?" Jacie asked in exasperation.

" 'Pretty me up'?" Hope spat. "God! I can't believe even *you* would say something that obnoxious."

Jacie swiveled in the driver's seat to face Hope directly. "Even me? What is that supposed to mean?"

"It means that you always find a way to make me feel like a loser!" Hope said, the words tumbling from her mouth in a garbled cry.

"So let me get this straight," Jacie said evenly. "I devote the whole day to making you feel special on your birthday, yet somehow I'm making you feel like a loser?"

"You know I'm hopeless!" Hope sobbed. "This is just your way of rubbing it in."

"You will stop at nothing to turn me into the bad guy!" Jacie said.

"You're the one who will stop at nothing to turn me into something I'm not," Hope said.

Jacie flung her hands in the air. "I don't want you to be something you're not! I just want you to be the best you that you can be."

"You sound like a shampoo commercial!"

Jacie exhaled angrily. "I don't get you," she muttered.

"No, you don't," Hope agreed. "You don't get that I'm not like you. You don't get that all the makeovers in the world won't turn me into a five-foot-nine blonde. I look like my mother and I always will!"

Hope cried into her hands, and Jacie was silent for a moment.

"I don't think I'm the one who isn't okay with that," Jacie finally said softly.

She waited a couple of minutes, then turned the key in the ignition and backed out of the parking lot. The hum of the engine was the only sound as they rode home. Hope wept quietly, rubbing tears from her eyes. With mascara streaming onto her cheeks, her makeover had lasted all of five minutes. She really was a loser.

"Stop at the mailbox," Hope barked as Jacie neared their home.

"Please?" Jacie prodded, but Hope was too angry for niceties, and Jacie sensed it. She pulled the car up beside the mailbox, and Hope opened it from the passenger window. She pulled out the contents and riffled through them impatiently. Bill, bill, bill, bill . . .

She dissolved into sobs all over again. "She didn't even send me a card!"

Jacie touched Hope's hair. "Oh, honey . . ."

"Not even a card on my birthday! I hate my mother!"

"I know, baby, I know."

Jacie pulled into the driveway, turned off the engine and sat there while Hope cried. Hope knew her stepmother couldn't do anything but be there. But she would be there. She always was.

• • •

"Hey, beautiful."

Hope's dad was speaking in barely a whisper as he creaked her bedroom door open and walked over to her bed. "Tough day?"

By the time he, Rob and Elizabeth had returned from the movie, Hope had been crying on her bed for an hour. Not only was any remnant of makeup long gone, but her eyes were red and puffy.

Hope nodded as her dad sat beside her and touched her cheek. "Want to tell me about it?"

A fresh well of tears sprang to her blue eyes. Her bottom lip quivered and she buried her face in the bedspread.

"Sweetie," her dad cooed. "Oh, sweetie."

Hope jerked herself into a sitting position. "She didn't even call!" she spat furiously. "Not a card, not a call . . . nothing! That's what I am to her. Nothing."

Sobs tumbled from her throat.

"Maybe she'll call later," her dad offered, but his voice had trailed off before he even finished the sentence. They both knew better.

In the first couple of years after Hope's parents' divorce, her mom, Bridget, had made halfhearted attempts to keep playing the mom role. But she was so angry at her ex-husband, Jack, particularly after the excruciating custody battle, and she was openly resentful during the snatches of time she was allotted with her daughter. It was as if she not only had lost a battle, but also had to play the humiliating role of being at the victor's beck and call. *Yes, you can see Hope this weekend, but only if you have her home in time for choir practice. No, you can't pick her up from school; you're not on the approved list. Quit feeding her peanuts; she's allergic.*

Bridget would spend their whole time together railing against the injustice of it all. Hope was her daughter, by God! Who was Jack to tell her what to feed her child, or whether she could pick her up from school? And she would appeal that ridiculous custody ruling. Jack knew the judge; the whole case was rigged.

That was when Hope's migraines had started. Hope wished her mother would find another boyfriend, like the one she had roomed with when she moved out of the house. But that relationship had lasted just a few months and only gave her more ammunition for hateful rants about men, about her lousy situation, about life in general. Hope grew to dread visits with her mother, but what she dreaded more was never seeing her again. That threat always loomed large.

"So he doesn't want you seeing me this weekend?" she'd spew to Hope. "Fine! I have a good mind to move to L.A.!"

And that was what she eventually did. At least, Hope *thought* she was in L.A. Bridget had moved there initially, but her long-sought acting career never panned out. As the calls and gifts grew more sparse, Hope lost track. Their last phone call had been when Bridget had heard through the grapevine that Jack was remarrying. Bridget screamed her fury into Hope's ear and pelted her with questions: What did Jacie look like? How long had they been dating? Who did Jack think he was, bringing this woman into her daughter's life without discussing the matter with Hope's own mother?

Hope's head started pounding midway through the conversation, which was also the approximate time that she began resenting Jacie. Her mom was right: Jacie was an interloper, an outsider. Without her in the picture, Hope's mom just might come back home. Stranger things had happened . . . hadn't they?

But her dad married Jacie anyhow, and her mom cut off contact. Even on Hope's birthday. Even on her birthday.

Her dad held her as she sobbed into his shirt.

"Why does Mom hate me?" she asked.

"She doesn't hate you," he responded, hugging her tighter. But he didn't even try to sound convincing. He never knew what to say. How do you explain why a mom drops off the face of the earth? There were no answers, no explanations. Hope had learned to quit talking about her . . . until now, when her emotions overflowed. All her dad could do was hold her.

At least she had her dad.

• • •

"You okay?"

Hope had long since dried her tears, but her head was hurting, so she stayed in her room the rest of the evening watching TV. Elizabeth tapped gingerly on her door around bedtime.

"I'm okay," Hope told her cousin, managing a smile. She propped herself up on an elbow. "How about you? Did you have fun with your dad?"

Elizabeth's mouth tightened. "I guess."

Hope sat up on her bed and motioned for Elizabeth to join her.

"Sorry I didn't get a chance to spend any time with Uncle Rob," Hope said. "I've been kind of . . . a mess today." She flipped a lock of hair dramatically. "And on my spa day!"

Elizabeth giggled, but then her brow knitted with concern. "I'm sorry your mom didn't call today."

Hope waved a hand absently through the air. "Who cares."

"You do," Elizabeth responded. "And I do, too."

Hope was silent for a moment, and Elizabeth rushed to fill the void. "Sometimes I wish my parents would just go away," she said.

"Really?"

Elizabeth shrugged. "Everything's just so . . . complicated, ya know?"

Hope brightened. "Complicated families. That's what bonds the Right-Under Club, remember?"

Elizabeth grinned. "Right."

Hope hugged her cousin. "Who knew there was an upside to complicated families?"

Hope's Right-Under Journal

Saturday, June 19

Happy birthday to me. I guess I'll sing that stupid song to myself since my mom blew me off. Again. I wonder if she even remembers it's my birthday. I wish I could forget her the way she's forgotten me. But how can I forget her when I see her face every time I look in the mirror? I know people are always telling kids, "You look just like your mom," even when they really don't. But there's no denying it: Mom and I look just alike. I wish I could have gotten a miracle makeover today. As in a whole new face and body. But I'm stuck with this one. I'm stuck being hopeless.

Tricia's Right-Under Journal

Sunday, June 20

Poor Hope. She, Elizabeth and Mei came over this afternoon, and while Troy was cooking burgers for us on the grill, she spilled the gory details about her spa day. Yikes! I thought the Right-Under advice was good, but it kinda blew up in her face. Sorry, Hope! I feel so sorry for her. A stepmother: YUCK! (And a prissy one at that! LOL) Thank heaven I don't have that problem. My dad would never remarry. He's way too cool for that kind of thing. He likes to stay light on his feet and keep his options open. But mostly, he's happiest when it's just the two of us. We're totally in sync, like we share the same brain. If it wasn't for my uptight mom, we'd be together all the time . . . or at least more often than one or two afternoons a month. Why is she so freaked out by how close we are? Shouldn't that make her happy? Is she worried about precious Troy feeling left out? Well, I feel left out all the time. In my own house! I wouldn't mind someone else catching a clue about what that's like. Dad's the only one who understands. But what can he do? My mom calls all the shots. He says she always has. Don't get me wrong . . . I love my mom. But I love my dad, too. What's so wrong with that?

11

"This third official meeting of the Right-Under Club will now commence."

Once again, Leighton had been late, but now everyone was accounted for as pink T-shirts filled the tree house.

"First, a belated happy birthday to Hope from anyone who hasn't seen her since the last meeting," Tricia said. Leighton yawned, tapping her fingertips rhythmically against her lips.

"And now on to old business," Tricia continued. She glanced at Mei. "We all know how fantastic Mei's mural turned out to be. Mei, how have things been going with your stepdad since then?"

"Okay," Mei said, folding her hands in her lap. "He's been bragging to everybody about my mural, which is nice. But it makes me a little nervous. Once school starts and people see it for themselves, they might think, This is what the principal's been raving about?"

"Trust us: nobody will think that," Tricia said.

Mei smiled. "Thanks. My mom likes it. She said I've inspired her to start painting again, as soon as the baby is born. Speaking of the baby, Mom's been having these contractions called Braxton Hicks, so the doctor thinks she might go into labor early."

"You'll need plenty of Right-Under advice once the baby is born," Tricia teased. "In fact, I'll give you some advance advice about changing diapers: let the adults do it."

The girls laughed, and Tricia turned her gaze to Hope.

"How about your spa day, Hope? How did it go?"

Hope rested her chin on her hands. "It was awful."

Leighton glanced from one Right-Under to another. They were all giving each other knowing looks. Hope's spa day was obviously old news to everyone but Leighton. She felt a pang. It made sense that Elizabeth already knew what was going on, since she was staying with Hope. And Mei was Hope's best friend. But Tricia? Hope had known Tricia only a few weeks. Leighton had known Hope forever. Yet Tricia knew and Leighton didn't. Leighton was out of the loop. So what else was new?

"What happened?" Leighton asked, tossing brown hair from her shoulder to seem as uninterested as possible.

"Ummmm . . ." Hope still didn't trust Leighton with sensitive information, and the other girls already knew about it. Still, Leighton was a Right-Under, and this was the point of the meetings. . . .

"It started out okay," Hope said tentatively. "I wasn't in the best mood, but I was going along with the program. Manicure, pedicure, facial, massage . . . But then Jacie said a couple of things that really ticked me off."

"What did she say?" Leighton asked, now clear of any doubt that she was the only one who didn't already know.

Hope pushed her curls back from her face. "Just her typical

remarks. You know . . . telling the makeup lady, 'We should take you home with us so you can pretty her up every day.' " The girls laughed at Hope's singsong imitation. "I felt like such a loser. And worse, I felt like that was the point."

"Why?" Leighton asked. "What is so bad about prettying yourself up? What's wrong with a little self-improvement?"

Again, she watched the other girls exchange glances.

"Hope just wants to be herself," Tricia said softly.

"You can be yourself and still brush your hair!" Leighton said.

Hope stared down at her hands.

"We're here to be supportive, remember?" Tricia said to Leighton.

"Looking great doesn't come as easily to everyone as it does to you," Hope said bitterly.

"But everyone can try." Leighton sniffed.

"Hope is prettier than you'll ever be!" Mei blurted out, surprising even herself with her anger. "And she's also pretty on the inside, where it counts. Maybe that can be *your* next self-improvement project."

Mei glared at Leighton, who stared back with narrowed eyes. But Leighton's heart sank. Why was everyone so mad at her? Why didn't the Coolest Girl in School ever really fit in?

Tricia cleared her throat loudly. "Okay, okay," she said. "We don't have to agree about everything, but the Right-Under Code says we have to support each other. And besides, Hope wasn't finished with her story yet. Hope?"

Hope shot a scathing look at Leighton, then stared back at her hands. "I got really mad at Jacie," she said. "I screamed at her in the car on the way home. But then we got back to the house, and as usual, she had, like, a gazillion presents for me, and I know she meant well. And maybe now she has a better idea of how small she can make me feel."

Hope skipped the part about her mother blowing off her birthday. That, even Mei didn't know.

"Do you think Jacie will stop trying to gussy you up?" Tricia asked.

Hope smiled. "Probably not. I still get 'the look' when she doesn't like my outfit, and new beauty products have a way of suddenly appearing on my dresser. I think she's bought every hair defrizzer on the market. And just for the record: none of them work."

The girls laughed.

"But . . . ," Hope continued, "her heart's in the right place."

"I like Aunt Jacie," Elizabeth said hesitantly, anxious not to distance herself from the others the way Leighton always managed to do but still compelled to defend her aunt. "She's really nice. I'm sad she makes you feel bad about yourself, but I know she doesn't mean to."

Tricia nodded. "Everybody I know thinks Troy is the greatest guy in the world. And he is nice. But when some random adult that your mom or dad happened to marry is suddenly judging you, or telling you what to do, or telling you how to be, or even just being in your space . . . it can be hard."

The girls nodded. If they had nothing else in common, they all understood that.

Tricia held the Problem Stick aloft. "I think we're ready to move on to the next problem."

Hope locked eyes with Elizabeth and gave her a prodding look. Elizabeth hesitated, but Tricia was already handing her the stick. "Elizabeth? Do you need the Problem Stick this week?"

Elizabeth blushed but took the stick and stood up. "It's not that big a problem," she began, but Hope's expression was urging her on. "And there's probably not any way for you to help me. . . ."

"Elizabeth!" Hope scolded.

"Okay, okay. I'm supposed to go to my grandparents' farm tomorrow and stay for ten days."

Leighton gave an exaggerated yawn.

"I totally love my grandparents," Elizabeth said with emphasis, "but they treat me like I'm a baby, especially since my parents broke up last year. They rent little kiddy videos for me, and my grandpa thinks I'm still into taking tractor rides and jumping into haystacks. . . ."

"Hey, that sounds fun," Tricia said.

"Yeah?" Elizabeth said, her face brightening.

"Totally. I'd love that no matter how old I was."

Elizabeth smiled appreciatively. Tricia always seemed to make people feel better. "It is pretty fun. But I'm having such a good time at Hope's house . . . so much fun with you guys." She blushed, knowing she was more like a little-kid interloper than an authentic member of the club, yet still . . .

"We've having fun with you, too," Tricia said. "And it's just ten days. The Right-Unders will still be here when you get back. You are coming back to Hope's house after your visit, right?"

"Sure she is," Hope said protectively. "She's staying until school starts." She put an arm around Elizabeth and squeezed her closer. Elizabeth suddenly felt like she might cry, but she willed herself not to. The last thing she wanted to do was act babyish.

"But in the meantime," Tricia said, "she has a problem. She needs suggestions for how to have a good time at her grandparents' house. Right-Unders, you know what to do."

"I don't," Leighton said. "I have no idea how to give somebody suggestions for making a trip to a farm bearable."

"Well, Old MacDonald," Hope said, "maybe your advice can be for Elizabeth to get adopted into a new family."

Leighton sneered.

"Everybody just think hard and do your best to help Elizabeth think of some ways to have fun with her grandparents," Tricia said. "Your time starts"—she glanced at her watch—"now."

Elizabeth settled more comfortably on the throw rug, relieved that all she had to do this time was sit and wait. She wondered if any spot on earth was cozier than this tree house. She wished she could live in it. She loved her new friends, even Leighton, whom she found more amusing than irritating. Elizabeth was only eleven, but she already knew that every group of girls seemed to have its Leighton, and the Leightons of the world were never quite as pulled together as they wanted other people to believe. Elizabeth wondered what Leighton was really like, under her perfect olive skin and sleek dark hair. She even felt a little sorry for her, though she wasn't sure why.

"Time's up," Tricia said, and the girls put down their pencils. Tricia passed the Solutions Bowl, and once again they folded their papers twice and put them in the bowl.

"My turn this time," Hope said cheerfully, but frowned slightly as Tricia resisted letting go of the bowl.

"Give it up, Tricia," Leighton snarled. Tricia reddened and handed Hope the bowl.

"Here we go," Hope said, unfolding and reading one piece of paper after another:

"SOLUTION: Do your grandparents live close to a mall? Tell them nothing would make you happier than daily shopping sprees.

"SOLUTION: Think of your visit like a camp. Learn new things to do on the farm. You'll stay busy and the time will fly by.

"SOLUTION: Bring all your own CDs and DVDs, then hole up in your room for some quality Elizabeth time.

"SOLUTION: Tell your grandparents things about your life that make them realize you're not a baby anymore. Ask your grandma to take you shopping for a bra!"

Elizabeth giggled at the last suggestion. Her grandparents might have been old, but they weren't blind. No way could she convince anybody she was ready for a bra. Still, she liked all the ideas . . . and she loved that the girls cared enough to try to help her.

"These are all really good suggestions," she said.

"I think the best thing you can do is combine these ideas," Tricia said decisively, still feeling a little prickly about losing the bowl. "Have some alone time, then hang out with your grandpa on the farm, then ask your grandma to take you shopping. . . . This might end up being really fun."

Elizabeth nodded. "My last night in town will be the Fourth of July, and Grandpa said they were taking me to a fireworks show," she said hopefully. "Maybe I'm worried for nothing."

Tricia took the Problem Stick back from her. "Go forth with the wisdom of the Right-Unders," she intoned dramatically.

"You'll miss our meeting next Thursday, but your report on your visit will be first on our agenda the meeting after that."

"I'll be ready," Elizabeth said, her cheeks glowing. "Thanks, guys."

Elizabeth's Right-Under Journal

Thursday, June 24

Hi, R.U. Journal. I may not have time to write for the next few days, so I thought I better check in. Today was my turn with the Problem Stick. So weird having my new friends focused on my little problem! R.U. ROCKS!!! They gave me really good advice, too. I can't wait to see how it turns out. But I'll miss them when I'm at my grandparents' house. Grandpa called after dinner to make sure I was all packed up. He and Grandma can't wait to see me. Grandma's got a cold, and Grandpa said her medicine is making her a little loopy (HIS WORD!) but they're still really excited about my visit. Grandparents. They live for this stuff. I love them, but I hope the next ten days fly by. I'LL MISS YOU, RIGHT-UNDERS!!!

12

"There's my girl!"

As Elizabeth stepped out of her uncle's car, her grandpa swept her into his broad, strong arms. Buck, his dog, yapped and jumped excitedly at his feet. Elizabeth extended a hand and let the dog lick it.

Hope, who had come along for the ride, got out of the car with her father.

"Hello, Mr. Carson," Hope's dad said. The two men shook hands.

"Jack, good to see ya," Elizabeth's grandpa said. "I really appreciate your driving Elizabeth over. And keeping her this summer . . . that's a real big help. I know my daughter appreciates it. It's giving her a chance to sort things out with your brother."

"We enjoy having Elizabeth with us," Hope's dad said.

"And who might this be?" Elizabeth's grandpa said to Hope.

"I'm Hope," she said, blushing.

"Not a chance! Elizabeth's cousin, Hope, is a scrawny little gal. You're a beautiful young woman!"

Hope smiled and kissed his stubbly cheek.

"If you'd like to stay with Elizabeth during her visit," he told Hope, "we've got plenty of room."

Elizabeth looked excited, but Hope quickly shook her head. "I've got to get back home," she said. "Busy, busy, busy." She could have kicked herself. How lame did that sound?

Jack pulled Elizabeth's suitcase out of the trunk of his car. "Shall I take this inside for you?" he asked, but Elizabeth's grandpa was already taking it.

"No, no. I've got it," he said. "Jean would love to have you in for a glass of iced tea, but she's getting over a bad cold."

"No problem," Jack said. "I told the boss I'd be in the office by noon. But please give her our best. We need to head on back."

"Well then, drive safely," Mr. Carson said.

Hope hugged Elizabeth tightly. "Just ten days," she whispered into her ear. "Remember the Right-Unders' advice. And have a great time."

"I'll try," Elizabeth whispered back.

Jack and Hope got in the car and drove away, leaving a dust trail in their wake. The farmhouse was large, comfortable and modern, but the grounds—including the dirt driveway—spelled "country" loud and clear. Elizabeth had loved everything about the farm until recently. Now she found it vaguely embarrassing. She shook the thought from her head, ashamed of herself, and followed her grandpa into the house.

"Grandma?" she called as they stepped through the front door.

"Is that my girl?"

Elizabeth's grandmother, a thin woman with meticulously groomed gray hair, rushed into the foyer. "Oh . . . oh . . . ," she said, then hugged her granddaughter. She smelled of lilacs.

"Hi, Grandma."

"Yes . . . yes!"

Her grandpa cleared his throat. He suddenly looked old and tired. "Let's get you situated, young lady," he said, and Elizabeth followed him to the bedroom she used during visits. It was her mom's old room.

"Grandma, are we having meat loaf tonight?" Elizabeth called to her grandmother. Meat loaf on the first night of a visit was a tradition.

"Meat loaf . . . ," her grandmother mumbled.

"Your grandma's not feeling so well," her grandfather said haltingly. "How about we go out for pizza tonight?"

"What's wrong with Grandma?" Elizabeth asked anxiously.

"Why, not a thing, unless your grandpa's going to make a federal case about my little cold," her grandma said, walking into the room in her breezy, graceful way. Elizabeth felt a flood of relief.

"Pizza sounds great," she said.

"What about my meat loaf?" her grandma asked, her eyes darting from one to the other.

"We'll have your meat loaf later in the week, honey," her grandpa told her gently. "Elizabeth, I could sure use some help on the tractor today."

Elizabeth grinned. Her "help" amounted to riding by his side, but right now, that suited her just fine.

"Back soon, Grandma," she called as she followed her grandfather out the door.

They took the dirt path to the tractor outside the barn. Grandpa hoisted Elizabeth into the passenger seat and off they went, enveloped in the clean, fresh scent of wheat and grass. "My tomatoes are doing fine this summer," her grandpa said, pulling close enough to a vine to pluck one off and hand it to Elizabeth. She wiped it on her shirt and took a bite, laughing when the juice trickled down her chin.

"Elizabeth, your grandma . . . ," her grandfather said as he drove, still staring straight ahead.

"Yes?"

"She's . . ."

Elizabeth's hand froze, the half-eaten tomato midway to her mouth. "She's what? What's wrong with Grandma, Grandpa?"

Her grandfather glanced at her from the corner of his eye, then smiled. But the smile didn't make it to his eyes. "She's fine, just fine," he said. "We're just both getting older."

Elizabeth swallowed hard. Her grandfather reached over and squeezed her knee. "Honey, everything's fine," he insisted. "Just bear with us old folks. Sometimes, when you get older, you . . ."

Elizabeth didn't know what to think. Why wasn't her grandfather finishing his sentences? That wasn't his style at all. Why was he being so weird?

"Can I pick some tomatoes, Grandpa?" she said, suddenly feeling unbearably restless on the tractor. "I need to stretch my legs."

"Good idea," he said. "And I don't even have to pay you!"

"I never said that," she teased. He stopped the tractor and handed her a burlap sack from the floor of the tractor.

"How about I join you at the crick in half an hour or so and we'll kick up our heels together?"

She giggled at her grandfather's pronunciation of "creek."

"See you at the crick," she said genially, then starting plucking bright red tomatoes off the vines.

After a while, her sack was getting uncomfortably heavy.

She headed toward the creek, hearing Buck's gleeful bark and the bossy *bwack* of chickens in the distance.

She took off her shoes and sat on a tree-shaded bank, dipping her feet into the cold, clear water of the creek.

"Save some of that water for me," her grandfather called from behind her. He walked over, kissed the top of her head and sat beside her.

"So, missy," he said, "I think you've grown a foot since Christmas. You better not wait so long between visits next time. I might not know who you are, and then I'm liable to pepper you with my shotgun when you pull up in the driveway."

She smiled and plucked a dandelion from the ground. "I'm still short," she said, feigning grouchiness.

"Oh, you'll be nice and tall like your mama," her grandfather said. "You wait and see. Ya miss your mom?"

Elizabeth squinted at him through the glare of the midday sunshine. She wasn't used to her grandpa's asking questions about feelings. She was used to his asking questions like whether she'd fed the chickens.

"Yeah, but I've been having fun at my cousin's house," she said, blowing the dandelion tufts into the breeze.

"But you like living with your mom . . . right?"

Elizabeth subtly shrank away from her grandfather. She knew where this was heading. "Sure," she said coolly. "She's my mom."

"Right you are," her grandpa said. "She's your mother, and every child belongs with her mother. Don't let anybody tell you any different."

Elizabeth felt a thud in her stomach. The nicest thing about being at Hope's house for the past few weeks had been her distance from the words she'd grown to hate: "Divorce." "Lawyers." "Custody." Sure, she missed her mom . . . and her dad . . . but she didn't miss their problems. And why did their problems have to be hers? It wasn't fair.

Her grandpa suddenly jerked his foot forward, splashing Elizabeth with creek water.

"Hey!" she yelped.

"Hey yourself, sissy!" he teased. "What are you, some kind of city slicker who can't take a little crick water?"

"I'll show you crick water!" she said, lowering herself into the creek and using both hands to splash him.

Her grandpa laughed and hopped in, too. Soon, they were a mass of flailing arms and legs, splashing each other merrily. Elizabeth resisted the sprays of water at first, squealing and shielding her face. But then she surrendered.

"Here goes nothing!" she announced, tipping her body sideways. She fell like a plank into the cool, clear water.

• • •

"What in the world did he do to you?" Elizabeth's grandmother asked as she walked onto the front porch, soaked from head to toe, her teeth chattering. Her grandmother had seen her through the window and brought her a towel. Elizabeth accepted it gratefully.

"We were playing in the creek," she explained.

Her grandmother narrowed her eyes at her husband. "What were you thinking, old man?" she demanded.

Elizabeth loved hearing her grandmother's scolding tone. The feeling of relief she'd had earlier in the day came flooding back.

"It was her idea!" her grandfather insisted, grabbing the towel from Elizabeth and patting himself dry.

"Hey!"

All three of them laughed.

"Now, Margaret, you scoot right inside the house and change into some dry clothes," said her grandma.

The laughter halted.

Elizabeth looked at her grandfather, who looked nervously at his wife.

"You called Elizabeth by her mother's name, honey," he said. Her grandma's eyes skittered fretfully. "Elizabeth," she muttered, but more to herself than to either of them.

"Elizabeth," Elizabeth's grandpa affirmed. "Elizabeth's spending some time with us, honey."

Anger flashed across her grandmother's face. "Of course she is! What do I look like, a fool?"

More uncomfortable silence.

"I'm gonna go change clothes," Elizabeth said, then hurried inside.

She went into her mother's old bedroom, tossed her wet clothes on the floor and pulled on a dry shirt and shorts.

What was going on? Why were her grandparents acting so weird? It had been only a few months since she'd seen them last. How could they . . . could she . . . have changed so much in such a short time? She lay on the bed and shivered.

"Elizabeth?"

It was her grandmother's voice, calling her from outside the door.

"Yes, Gram."

"You okay, honey?" her grandma asked, opening the door slowly.

"I'm fine."

"Well . . ." Her grandma wrung her hands and stared at them intently. "I'll be making my meat loaf later on."

Elizabeth paused. "I thought Grandpa said we were going out for pizza."

"Pizza . . . pizza." Her grandma lowered her head to peer more closely at her hands. "Pizza . . ."

She walked out the door and down the hallway.

Tears brimmed in Elizabeth's eyes, but she squeezed them away as she heard her grandpa's heavy footsteps making their way to her room.

"Elizabeth?" he asked, looming in the doorway like a friendly bear.

"What's the matter with Grandma?" Elizabeth asked abruptly. She was afraid to hear the answer, yet she was more afraid not to.

"A cold. Just a cold that's hard to shake." He averted his eyes.

They both paused as they heard Elizabeth's grandma call them from the kitchen. "I'll be making my meat loaf later on," she said, her thin voice lilting down the hallway.

Elizabeth's eyes leveled an unspoken accusation at her grandfather, and he finally looked at her.

"She doesn't sound like she has a cold."

"She's gettin' on in years, honey," he said quietly.

"She called me Margaret. She's forgetting things." Elizabeth swallowed hard. "Is it Alzheimer's?"

Her grandfather was silent for a moment but held her gaze. "We think so."

Elizabeth burst into tears and crumpled onto the bed, curling her body into a fetal position. Her grandpa rushed over and held her.

"Honey, honey," he cooed. "It's not the end of the world. Grandma's still a spry old gal. She hasn't left us yet. And it may not even be that ol' nasty A-word. The docs say different medicines can cause confusion. They're doing some experimenting, and . . . and . . ."

And her grandma had Alzheimer's disease. They both knew it. They had watched her grandma's sister, Emma, go through the same thing a year earlier. It started with her forgetting words—they'd be right on the tip of her tongue but somehow she couldn't form them. After a while, she started to repeat herself. Then she would call people by the wrong names, by the names of relatives who had been dead for years. Toward the end, she would go to the grocery store and get lost coming home. It was depressingly familiar. Emma had been in the nursing home only a couple of months or so when she stopped recognizing any of them. Thank heaven she hadn't lived long after that. Her decline was so sudden, so crushing. Elizabeth knew the disease all too well. Her whole family did.

"Does Mom know?" she asked through sobs.

Her grandpa held her tighter. "She has enough on her plate right now," he responded. "Like I said, the docs don't even have a definite diagnosis yet. When there's news to tell, I'll tell it."

"I want my mother," Elizabeth sobbed.

"Now, honey," her grandpa said. "I'll take good care of you, I promise. And your grandma's okay most of the time. You don't have to be scared."

But Elizabeth was scared. Her fear felt like a dark, heavy blanket descending over her face. She wondered if that was how it felt to her grandma. She wondered if she could bear to watch her grandma slip away.

13

Elizabeth's grandpa was wrong. Her grandma wasn't okay most of the time.

By the end of their first day together, Elizabeth knew that confusion was seriously clouding her grandmother's mind. Yet her grandma was as kind and loving as ever. Elizabeth had allowed herself to wallow in despair that first night, but she woke up the next morning with a sense of purpose. She probably didn't have much time left with her grandmother. She wanted to make it count. Her grandma had always been there for her. It was time to return the favor.

Elizabeth got out of bed and pulled on jeans and her R.U. T-shirt. Technically, the shirt was supposed to be reserved for Right-Under meetings, but she needed a symbol of moral support today. She'd had a feeling it might come in handy. The girls would understand.

She pulled a brush through her loose blond curls, brushed her teeth in the bathroom adjoining her bedroom, then walked briskly down the hall into the kitchen. She could hear her grandmother making breakfast.

"Hi, Grandma," Elizabeth said, giving her a hug. "The bacon smells good."

Her grandma looked startled, but only for a moment.

"Good morning, sleepyhead."

Now, that sounded familiar. On a farm, a seven-thirty wake-up time was considered late.

"Is Grandpa already outside?"

Her grandmother's eyes flashed irritation. "Of course he is," she snapped, as if Elizabeth had lobbed a trick question.

Elizabeth blushed and sat at the kitchen table. "Just asking," she mumbled.

"He's always in the fields by daybreak this time of year," her grandmother said, but more to herself than to Elizabeth.

"Right," Elizabeth said.

Her grandma shook her head as if clearing the thought, then asked, "Who's ready for bacon and eggs?"

"I'd love some. Thanks."

She watched her grandma transfer the contents of a frying pan and a griddle onto a plate and hand the plate to Elizabeth. She returned the empty frying pan and griddle to the stove.

"Grandma, you need to turn the burners off," Elizabeth said gently.

Her grandmother's eyes darted again, then registered flashes of emotion that Elizabeth couldn't identify. "Yes," she finally said, and turned the knobs. "Yes."

As heartbreaking as the thought was, Elizabeth realized that it probably wasn't safe for her grandmother to be alone. Should she talk to her grandpa? Her mom? She wasn't sure. That decision could wait until later. She had an awful lot to think about all of a sudden.

Elizabeth smoothed her shirt and bit into a crisp piece of bacon.

"R-U," her grandmother mused aloud, staring at the shirt. "Are you what?"

Elizabeth laughed, and her grandmother laughed back. "It's a club shirt," Elizabeth said. "Hope and I are part of a club."

"Ah . . . ," her grandmother said. "Hope . . ."

"Right," Elizabeth said. "My cousin, Hope. Jack's daughter. Jack is my dad's brother."

"Jack . . ." Her grandma's eyebrows arched. "Yes, Jack."

Elizabeth bit off another piece of bacon. "Hey, Grandma," she said. "I have an idea."

"An idea?"

Elizabeth nodded. "I went to a scrapbooking party a few weeks ago. It was fun. You can buy kits, or you can collect odds and ends around the house and gather your own supplies."

"Supplies?"

"Construction paper, stencils, notions from a sewing kit . . . that kind of thing."

Her grandmother's brow knitted.

"You make a scrapbook with your supplies," Elizabeth explained. "You pull together family photos, postcards, certificates from school . . . and make them look pretty on the paper. You put the pieces of paper in transparent sheets, then put the sheets in a binder. Then you've got a scrapbook."

"I know what a scrapbook is," her grandmother said testily.

"The point isn't just to have a scrapbook," Elizabeth said. "The point is to get together with friends and make a scrapbook."

"So your generation invented scrapbooks, huh?" her grandma

said wryly. Elizabeth loved hearing her sound sarcastic. That was Grandma.

"Let's make a scrapbook together," she said, standing up and putting an arm around her grandmother's small waist.

"We're going to make a . . ." Grandma's voice trailed off.

"A scrapbook," Elizabeth said firmly. "You and I are going to make a scrapbook. It'll be our project during my visit. Grandpa can take us to the store for supplies, and meanwhile, you and I can start pulling together some old pictures. And I brought my digital camera, so we can take some new ones, too."

Her grandma's face turned taut with worry. "Have you had your breakfast?" she asked anxiously.

Elizabeth nodded and rubbed her stomach. "Yep. Just finished. It was good. Thanks. Now, our project," she reminded her patiently.

"Yes," her grandma repeated, "our project."

Elizabeth wasn't sure how much of her grandmother's memory she could salvage in a scrapbook, but she was determined to give it her best shot. For both of their sakes.

• • •

Elizabeth was so goofy for the rest of the morning that her grandmother couldn't help laughing, even if sometimes she wasn't sure what she was laughing about. Elizabeth was prompting her grandma to make silly faces for the camera, and she was taking pictures of the oddest things . . . her grandma's pearls, the telephone, the remote control.

"What has gotten into you, Margaret?" her grandmother asked. Elizabeth pushed past the awkwardness. She was having too much fun to let her grandma's cloudy moments put a damper on their day. Besides, she was on a mission. She remembered the things that her Great-aunt Emma first began forgetting: a name, a phone number, a word. Elizabeth was determined to ease her grandma's passage into this murky world, and maybe the scrapbook would buy her just a little bit of time.

"We're putting a picture of my glasses in the scrapbook?" her grandma asked as Elizabeth propped them on the table, stepped back a couple of feet, then snapped the picture.

"Humor me, Grandma," Elizabeth said. "I'm quirky."

They walked around the farm taking pictures, too . . . the dog, the chickens, a dogwood tree, a tomato vine. . . . The more Elizabeth thought about what she might want to capture in the scrapbook, the more purposeful she became. Elizabeth's grandmother seemed a little disoriented outside, but the longer they walked through the grass and along the dirt trails, the more comfortable she became.

As they headed for the barn, Elizabeth saw her grandfather walking toward them holding a bag of mulch. "What are you gals up to?" he asked, seeming pleased to see his wife in the sunshine.

"Taking pictures," Elizabeth said. "Smile!"

He pulled his wife into the frame and playfully tickled her as he wrapped his arm around her thin waist. Their silly grins made Elizabeth feel lighter on her feet as she snapped their picture.

"What are the pictures for?" her grandpa asked.

"Grandma and I are making a scrapbook," Elizabeth explained. "I'll need to print the photos. Can you take us to the store?"

"I'll go you one better than that," her grandpa said. "Your

mom gave us a fancy printer for Christmas to go with the computer that I still don't know how to turn on. Finally, it'll get used!"

Elizabeth giggled. "I'll teach you how to use it. But we need some other supplies, too. Just a quick trip into town?"

"Ready when you are," he said cheerfully.

"We're ready now," Elizabeth said, then walked with her grandparents to their truck. Her grandpa opened the passenger door and gently hoisted his wife up first, then Elizabeth. She'd taken many rides with them in this truck, but this was the first time she hadn't sat in the middle. Her grandma seemed so small sitting there.

Her grandfather surprised her by slipping a CD into a player in the dashboard.

"You have CDs, Grandpa?" she asked.

"Duh!" he responded, making them all laugh with his teen-speak. "Just last week, I traded in my hi-fi, with its woofers and tweeters. I'm hip with the scene."

Elizabeth's hair blew in the wind as she rested her elbow on the open window. "Yeah, you're one cool dude, Grandpa," she said, staring out at the green pastures and neat rows of crops.

As the CD started, he and her grandma sang along. It was an old song, one Elizabeth had heard them sing countless times together: *"I'll be loving you always, with a love that's true always."*

Her grandpa sang the melody, her grandma the harmony. Her grandma's voice had a bit of vibrato; her grandpa's was firm and steady. They sounded beautiful together. One song after another they sang together. Her grandmother's memory of the lyrics was flawless.

How does she remember words to zillion-year-old songs but forget my name? Elizabeth thought wistfully, but she didn't dwell on the notion. Her time with her grandmother was too limited to spend it questioning things she would probably never understand. Right now, it was time to enjoy the music.

• • •

"There's Grandpa."

It was the picture Elizabeth had taken of him earlier in the day by the barn. She used a glue stick to paste his picture on a piece of lime green construction paper. She traced the outline in glue and sprinkled silver glitter on the border.

"FRANK," she wrote in neat letters with a fine-point marker by his picture. "Birthday: October 23. Job: Farmer. Favorite foods: Meat loaf and broccoli."

Elizabeth's grandma peered closer at her handiwork. "This is how people make scrapbooks nowadays?" she asked.

Elizabeth nodded. "Yep."

"Very literal," her grandmother observed.

Elizabeth filled one page after another: pictures of her, her mother, their relatives and friends, all with neatly printed details. Then came the pictures of her grandma's possessions.

"Remote control," Elizabeth wrote. "Stays on coffee table in front of couch. Turns TV off and on."

"*Very* literal," her grandmother murmured again.

It was moments like those that made Elizabeth turn and stare hard into her grandmother's eyes. Sometimes she seemed so normal. Was Elizabeth overreacting? Maybe her grandfather was right. . . . Her grandma was perfectly fine, just having a few fleeting memory problems because her medicines were interacting in some weird way.

But no. As the week wore on, Elizabeth knew better, and so did her grandfather, deep down. She could tell by the way he averted his eyes every time her grandmother got confused. And whenever her grandma did show traces of her old personality—her wit, her cleverness, her intelligence—a sheer veil seemed to descend over her eyes in the very next breath, when she was once again calling Elizabeth by the wrong name, or asking what in the world Elizabeth was doing there in the first place, or asking whether they should have meat loaf for dinner an hour after the table had been cleared.

For the first couple of days, Elizabeth's brow would knit anxiously at these moments. Sometimes her grandma noticed and seemed scared or angry, demanding to know what was wrong. So Elizabeth stopped reacting, for both her grandma's sake and her own. Her grandma's illness was what it was. Elizabeth was getting better at rolling with the punches. Her parents had given her plenty of practice the past year.

She and her grandma settled into a pattern. Every morning after her grandpa went into the fields, she and her grandmother would amble around the farm, taking more pictures: a rake, a caterpillar, a rainbow. . . . Then they would go inside, Elizabeth would print out the pictures and she and her grandma would add them to their scrapbook.

"Who's that?" her grandmother asked her one afternoon as Elizabeth pasted in a picture of her grandma as a young girl, beaming in a cream-colored dress with a wide sash that hung loosely around her hips, and an impossibly big matching bow in her hair.

"That's you," Elizabeth responded, affixing gold stars at each corner of the picture.

"Me?" her grandma said, laughing lightly.

"You look like you were around my age in this picture," Elizabeth said. "What were you like when you were a kid?"

"Let's see . . . ," her grandma said. Her eyes squinted in concentration, then fell back on the picture. "Who's that?" she asked again, pointing to the same picture.

"That's you," Elizabeth responded patiently. "Tell me what you were like when you were my age."

"Your age . . ." More squinting. Elizabeth could almost see her struggling to open different windows in her brain. This time, the window was nudged open. "I liked to skate!" her grandma said brightly. "I was good, too. We would ice-skate on the frozen pond in the winters. Once, the ice broke and my brother had to fish me out. Oooh, it was so cold! My mother told me I could never ice-skate again, but I sneaked off to do it anyway. I loved it too much to stop. If I fell in again, well, so be it."

Elizabeth laughed. This memory seemed fresher in her grandma's mind than her recollection of the meal they'd finished fifteen minutes earlier.

"Were you good in school?" Elizabeth asked.

"Not in math," her grandmother responded with no hesitation. "I never understood math, and I had a horrible math teacher—Miss Holloway—who delighted in humiliating me and making me feel like an idiot. But I was good in other subjects. My penmanship was flawless. And I won a spelling bee. 'Accentuate': *a-c-c-e-n-t-u-a-t-e*. 'Accentuate.' "

Elizabeth clapped her hands lightly. "I won a spelling bee, too. 'Colloquial': c-o-l-l-o-q-u-i-a-l: 'Colloquial.' "

Her grandma's eyes danced, and she clapped for Elizabeth. "You're a fine speller, Margaret," she said.

Elizabeth's eyes softened as she looked dreamily into her grandmother's eyes. "Thanks, Grandma."

• • •

"I've got a surprise for you, honey."

Elizabeth's grandpa's eyes twinkled as he gently shook her awake the next morning.

She stretched her arms and sniffed fresh linen. Whatever else her grandma couldn't remember, she never forgot to wash and line-dry Elizabeth's sheets regularly. "What's up, Grandpa?"

"Grandma has a doctor's appointment today," he said. "Your mom wants to come with us, so she'll be here in a little while."

Elizabeth sat up. "You told Mom?"

He shrugged. "She knows your grandma's been forgetful lately. We had a nice long talk on the phone last night." He forced a smile. "I think we're all on the same page now, honey."

Elizabeth swallowed hard. She was glad her mom knew, but it made her grandma's condition more real. She understood her grandpa's urge to push the problem away as long as he could, but there was no pushing it away anymore. Tears sprang to her eyes.

"Honey, honey," her grandpa cooed, sweeping her into a hug. "It's just a doctor's appointment, that's all. No big deal. Which leads me to the surprise."

Elizabeth's eyebrows arched.

"I figured you wouldn't want to spend half the day sitting in a waiting room with us old folks," he said. "So your uncle Jack and aunt Jacie are driving over today with your friends."

The corners of her mouth crept into a smile.

"Jacie says you've cooked up some kind of club," her grandpa continued. "Looks like the clubhouse is moving to the farm today."

"They're all coming?" Elizabeth asked brightly. "Hope and Tricia? And Mei? Even Leighton?"

Her grandpa nodded. "Jacie said she rounded up the whole bunch. They'll be here in an hour or so. You can swim in the crick, feed the chickens, jump in the hay . . . you can even teach your friends how to milk a cow!"

Elizabeth laughed, then turned somber.

"I think I should go with you to the doctor," she said.

"Oh, do you, now?" her grandpa asked playfully. "You think ol' Grandpa's gonna take a wrong turn and end up taking Grandma to Las Vegas? Hey, that's not a bad idea. . . ."

Elizabeth smiled. "I may not be much help, but I could . . . I don't know . . . hold Grandma's hand or something if she's nervous."

Her grandpa leaned closer to Elizabeth's face. "You leave the hand-holding to me," he said softly. "In fact, you leave everything to me. Your job today is to have fun with your friends."

Elizabeth nodded. That she could manage.

• • •

"Eeeewww!"

Leighton shooed away the chicken that abruptly flapped its wings in her face as she squatted to get a better look.

"Get him away from me!" she shrieked.

"He's a she," Elizabeth said calmly, luring the chicken away with a trail of feed.

"What was I thinking, coming to Old MacDonald's Farm?"

Leighton said, but her tone was light. After spending the morning soaring in tire swings, eating tomatoes straight off the vine, climbing trees and riding bikes on dusty dirt trails, even she had to admit that farm life wasn't half bad. Until they visited the chicken coop, that is.

"How can you stand this smell?" Leighton asked, wrinkling her nose and wiping dirty hands on the back of her cutoffs.

"You mean the smell of fresh air?" Hope's dad teased.

"I'm with Leighton," Jacie said, waving a hand in front of her nose.

"It smells better inside the house," Elizabeth acknowledged, reveling in her role as hostess and farm expert. Her cheeks hadn't stopped glowing since her uncle Jack's car had pulled in the driveway three hours earlier. It was awesome seeing her friends tumble out of the car, their ponytails swishing as they ran to embrace Elizabeth.

"There's a pot of chili on the stove," she said as she scattered the rest of the chicken feed. "Anybody ready for lunch?"

The girls' arms shot into the air. They had definitely worked up an appetite.

"Just one more chore first," Elizabeth said, leading her visitors to the barn. She grabbed a bucket and stool, patted the back of a cow and positioned the stool underneath.

"Tell me you are not touching those things," Leighton said, pointing to the cow's teats and cringing.

"Okay," Elizabeth said agreeably. "You do it."

Leighton's jaw dropped. "Not in this lifetime."

"I'll do it!" Tricia volunteered. "But you'll have to show me how. And you'll have to promise that Bessie won't get mad and kick me. Or bite me. Or whatever."

"Her name's Zelda," Elizabeth corrected her. "Grandpa named her after some famous writer's crazy wife because Zelda is a little . . . unpredictable sometimes."

Tricia presented the palms of her hands and backed away. "Changed my mind."

"Oh, she's really sweet," Elizabeth insisted. "And you can't visit a farm without milking a cow. Everybody can take a turn."

"Everybody but me," Jacie said nervously.

"And me." Leighton surveyed her nails. "I don't want to mess up my manicure."

"Chickens!" Elizabeth goaded. "*Bwack! B-b-b-bwack!*" The girls laughed as she jutted her chest out and flapped her arms.

"Well . . . ," Mei said nervously, "you start and show us how to do it."

Elizabeth positioned the bucket and grabbed two teats, pumping them rhythmically one by one. Soon, milk began flowing into the bucket.

"Cool," Tricia said, leaning closer for a better look.

"Here," Elizabeth said. "Your turn."

Tricia hesitated for a second, then grabbed the teats as Elizabeth eased off the stool. Zelda looked bored.

"Wow," Tricia said as the milk flowed. "I'm really doing it!"

"My turn!" Hope said, replacing Tricia on the stool. She grimaced as she took the teats, but soon relaxed. She started an impromptu rap to the rhythm of her hands:

"Now, Zelda's givin' milk and it's just as smooth as silk.
She doesn't even mind, 'cause I'm doin' really fine.
This farmin' is alarmin' but it's charmin' in a way.
I'm milkin' it for all it's worth—a farmin' girl today."

Midway through the rap, the girls were clapping, swaying their hips and twirling happily on the hay-covered floor. Hope invented a second verse to keep the mood alive:

"Don't worry if you spill it, 'cause the cow will just refill it.
Yeah, Zelda aims to please, so I'm giving her a squeeze.
This farm work's kinda icky but I'm really not that picky.
The cow can take a bow. I got the hang of this, and how!"

The girls applauded appreciatively.

"Hope!" Jacie said. "How did you do that off the top of your head? Oh, my gosh . . . you're amazing!"

Hope locked eyes with her stepmother and smiled.

"Mei's turn," Elizabeth said, nudging a reluctant Mei toward Zelda.

"Do I have to?" Mei asked in a squeaky voice.

"Only if you want to eat lunch. You can do it."

Elizabeth guided Mei's hands as she replaced Hope at the stool.

"Easy, Bessie," Mei said nervously. "I mean Zelda." She giggled as she gently pumped the teats.

"Uncle Jack, you want a turn?" Elizabeth asked.

"I'll pass," he said with a broad grin. "Looks like you girls have this situation firmly under control."

"Aunt Jacie?"

"Pass," she said quickly.

"That leaves you, Leighton," Elizabeth said. "Don't worry about your manicure. Zelda won't bite your nails off, I promise." She figured she'd have to shove Leighton over to the cow, but to her surprise, Leighton approached Zelda willingly.

"Might as well," she said coolly.

She traded places with Mei and squeezed her eyes shut as she pumped.

"Eeeewww!" she said. "How do you turn her off?"

The girls laughed, at which point Leighton suddenly turned a teat upward and sprayed them with milk.

Leighton smiled with satisfaction as the girls shrieked and wiped milk off their faces.

"Told ya I'd get you back for dunking me into the pool!"

• • •

"What did the doctor say?"

Her friends' visit to the farm had been perfect, but now that they'd gone home, Elizabeth turned her attention back to her grandmother.

Her mom smoothed Elizabeth's hair as they sat together on the front porch swing. Crickets chirped as dusk settled. "Ummm . . . ," she said slowly, "it's probably Alzheimer's, honey."

Elizabeth's eyes fell. Her mom put a cool palm on her cheek. "It's okay," she insisted. "We'll take good care of her."

"She won't get any better?" Elizabeth asked in barely a whisper.

Her mom shook her head. "Medicines can slow things down a little, but no . . . she won't get better."

Tears trickled down Elizabeth's cheeks.

"Honey, I'm so sorry you had to find out this way," her mother said. "I didn't know either, or I would have prepared you. I should have known."

"Grandpa didn't want anybody to know," Elizabeth said.

"He didn't even want to know himself. I think he thought if he didn't say it out loud, it wouldn't be true."

"Still," her mother said, "I would have noticed, if I hadn't been so selfish the last few months."

"You haven't been selfish," Elizabeth said protectively.

Her mom looked deeply into her eyes. "Nobody knows better than you how selfish I've been," she said. "And I'm sorry, sweetie. It's just . . . I love you so much, and I'm so scared of losing you."

Now her mother's eyes were brimming with tears.

Elizabeth grasped her hand and squeezed it. "You won't lose me," she said.

Of course, she'd said the same thing to her dad. Her stomach roiled like boiling water.

"You know what?" her mother said, forcing a smile. "I'm the one who should be reassuring you. How does that sound for a change?"

Elizabeth couldn't deny that it sounded really good.

Leighton's Right-Under Journal

Wednesday, June 29

Here's a first: writing in a journal without having to. Oh, well. I never thought I'd spend a day on a farm, either. I guess this is a day for firsts. I didn't want to go. Mom made me. But go figeur. It was kind of a blast, not counting a few oders I'd rather forget. (P-U!!!!) Awsem news: I finally got the girls back for dunking me in the pool! I sprayed milk in their faces when I was milking the cow. LOL! Wheres a video camera when you need one? We laughed so hard, we cried. Usually I think they hate me, but every once in a wile, I feel like I acktially fit in. That's how I felt 2day, even tho I know they make fun of me behind my back. Jellus. Oh, well.

Today was really fun. Hope has been tutering me at the pool, so I hope I pass math next year. But it's hard. Nothing's really sticking. Hope thinks she's so brilient. Why can't she teach math? I wonder if I can use this journal for extra credit when school starts. Now, that's brillient! G2G. Scott's probably trying to IM me. Scottie's a Hottie! I LUV SCOTT. SCOTT + LEIGHTON 4 EVER. By 4 now.

• • •

HoPeLess has just signed on.

HoPeLess: Mei? R U there?

artsyMEI: Hi, Hope. Can U believe Leighton sprayed us with milk 2day? I still have milk in my nostrils! You gotta admit, she got us good.

HoPeLess: Now, let's not get carried away.

artsyMEI: Come on, Hope, cut Leighton some slack. She was actually fun 2day!

HoPeLess: So now she's your BFF?

artsyMEI: I didn't say that. I just said she wasn't totally annoying 4 a change. Hey . . . Elizabeth seems like she's having a good time on her grandparents' farm. All that worrying 4 nothing!

HoPeLess: I'm not so sure. I think something's wrong with her grandma.

Her mom called Jacie last night and they talked 4ever.

artsyMEI: If her grandma was sick, wouldn't Elizabeth have told us?

HoPeLess: I'm not sure what's going on. I

called her a little while ago and she said everything was fine. But Elizabeth says everything is fine when everything is NOT fine.

artsyMEI: Maybe she wants to tell us all together. Just remind her: We R There for Her. BTW: Can U come to the pool 2morrow? Tricia said she can make it, but she'll have to bring her little sister.

HoPeLess: OK. But if Leighton shows up, I might have an emergency stomachache.

artsyMEI: I can't stay long. I started a new art project. Stan asked me to paint the baby's room.

HoPeLess: O NO! Rainbows and butterflies?!?

artsyMEI: LOL. Stan told me to paint whatever I like. He said he trusts my instincts! I want to paint 3 walls green, then paint a tropical rain forest mural on the 4th wall.

HoPeLess: Awesome! That baby will have the coolest room in town.

artsyMEI: Technically, rain forests are hot and muggy—not cool. (Get it? ☺)

HoPeLess: Groan. Have fun painting. See you 2morrow at the pool.

LYLAS.

artsyMEI has signed off.

HoPeLess has signed off.

14

"*No floaties!*"

Tricia glanced apologetically at her friends. "Little sisters are so annoying."

She was trying to pull Hissy's hands through inflatable armbands, but the little girl was gearing up for an Olympic-scale tantrum.

"You can't swim without your floaties," Tricia said reasonably.

"*Noooo!*" Hissy's cheeks bulged like tomatoes.

"Girls!" Tricia's stepdad, Troy, called from a lounge chair. "What seems to be the problem?"

Your bratty daughter is the problem, Tricia thought, but kept her mouth shut.

"*No floaties!*" Hissy screeched again, in case anyone at the pool had missed it the first three times.

"Fine!" Tricia said through gritted teeth. "I don't want to take you swimming anyhow! Go sit with your dad and let me have fun with my friends."

"*Swim!*" Hissy wailed, reaching her pudgy arms toward Tricia.

"Tricia!" Troy scolded from his lounge chair. "You have to be gentle with the floaties. Are you hurting her? Are you okay, Everly, sweetie?"

Tricia glared in his direction. "Yes, sweetie, is your mean big sister causing you any discomfort?" she mocked to Hissy. "You know, the whole world revolves around you, and I live my life only to serve your needs, so anything I can do—anything at all—to make your world a better place, why, just let me know."

Hope and Mei giggled, causing Everly to laugh, too. Her tantrum had run its course; now she was happily pulling her arms through the floaties.

"Shouldn't your stepdad be at work?" Hope asked.

Tricia rolled her eyes. "He wanted to spend the afternoon with 'his girls.' Lucky me."

"Look at me, Daddy!" Hissy trilled as Tricia helped her down the pool steps into the water.

"There's my girl!" Troy called.

"I don't know why I take you anywhere," Tricia muttered to her sister. "You're like . . . insecticide, and the cute guys I'm trying to impress are the insects."

"Did I hear something about cute guys?"

The girls looked up and saw Leighton standing by the pool in a fuchsia bikini, surveying the scene coolly as she adjusted her sunglasses.

"Get in!" Mei said cheerily.

"Would you keep it down?" Leighton whispered. "God. You girls are so immature."

Hope tossed Tricia and Mei a knowing look. This was the real Leighton. The farm act hadn't fooled her. Any flickers of fun or unconceited behavior were mere aberrations.

"So," Leighton said, sounding bored. "Where are the cute guys?"

Tricia tossed her head toward the deep end, where several boys were wrestling playfully. "*They're* kinda cute," she whispered.

Leighton pushed her sunglasses to the top of her head and raised an eyebrow. "Those guys? I don't think so. What are they, like, thirteen? They're children."

"How about that guy? Is he more your speed?" Hope said, nodding toward an elderly man inching his way poolside with a cane.

She exchanged high fives with Mei and Tricia, who laughed appreciatively.

Leighton scowled. "Better not write him off. He might be your only hope for a boyfriend." She pulled a lock of hair behind her ear. "Have you girls ever even had a boyfriend?"

"Mei has a crush on . . . ," Hope blurted out, but was silenced by Mei's withering glance.

"Who?" Leighton asked.

Mei blushed and stared at the water. "Nobody," she said in barely a whisper.

"Right. So what's 'nobody's' name?" Leighton persisted.

Hope tightened her lips. What a bigmouth she was. Poor Mei. The last thing she wanted Leighton knowing was that she had a crush on her stepbrother.

"Nobody," Hope repeated firmly. "I was just ragging on her."

Leighton looked from face to face. "You all know," she said evenly. "Everybody knows but me."

"I don't," Tricia said defensively.

"Sure you do," Leighton said with a trace of bitterness. She jutted her chin out indignantly. "As if I even care. You girls go back to gossiping about your little crushes. Don't let me stop you."

She spun on a barefoot heel, walked toward a lounge chair and settled in, carefully repositioning her sunglasses. Of course she looked gorgeous. Of course she looked cool. The tears glistening in her eyes were her little secret.

• • •

"You missed a spot."

Mei's mom pointed to a spot on the wall, and Mei brushed over it with green paint. Both mother and daughter were covered head to toe in paint flecks, and the worn white sheets they'd spread on the floor were starting to look tie-dyed.

Mei was tired—she'd been painting for three hours now, ever since she'd returned from the pool in the middle of the afternoon—but she couldn't resist giggling at her mom. "You have paint on your cheek," she said.

"In that case, we better even things out." Her mom dabbed a fingertip of paint onto the other cheek. "Maybe I'll start a new makeup trend. Green blush."

"You shouldn't even be in here," Mei scolded gently. "Aren't paint fumes dangerous for pregnant women?"

Mei's mom laughed. "So now you're an authority on pregnant women?"

Mei shrugged. "I worry about you."

Her mom's brow knitted. She put her paintbrush back in the pan and tugged Mei's ponytail. "Thanks, honey, but I'm taking good care of both the baby and me. I promise."

Mei lifted her brush for another stroke, but her mom touched her arm lightly. "I worry about you, too, you know," she told her daughter.

“No, you don’t. All you care about is the new baby.” Mei meant it to sound playful, but it didn’t quite come out that way.

“Mei,” her mother said. “Put your paintbrush down for a minute.”

Uh-oh. Mei had said too much. “I want to hurry and finish the walls so I can start the mural tomorrow,” she said. She envisioned soaring trees, tangled vines, leaping monkeys, brightly colored birds and assorted furry creatures darting out of the underbrush.

“I just want to talk for a minute,” her mom insisted, then motioned for Mei to join her on the floor. Mei reluctantly followed her lead, stretching out her legs and leaning back on the palms of her hands.

“It’s exciting to be pregnant,” her mother began, choosing her words carefully, “almost as exciting as when I was pregnant with you. The first one’s always . . . special. Mei, you’re my baby, too.”

Mei blushed and lowered her eyes. Why hadn’t she kept her mouth shut?

“This baby is going to enrich all our lives,” her mom continued, “but nobody could ever take your place.”

Mei put her hands over her ears. “Mom!” she said, exasperated. “You don’t have to say this stuff. I know, I know: you’ll love us just the same, blah, blah, blah.”

Her mother shook her head. “No. I’ll love you just as much, but not the same. I’ll love each of you differently, like you love each of your friends differently. They’re all different people, and you have unique relationships with each of them.”

Mei peered at the paint flecks on the sheets. She thought of the intimacy she shared with Hope, almost like they could read each other's thoughts. Then there was Tricia, the new girl, who was so smart and reliable. Elizabeth was starting to seem like a little sister; Mei felt just as protective of her as Hope did. And Leighton . . . what could you say about Leighton? She smiled at the thought.

"I know you've had to make a lot of adjustments throughout your life," her mom said softly. "Your dad dying . . ."

"I don't even remember that," Mei said.

"I know, honey, but you still had to deal with it, and it's affected your life ever since. Then having a new stepfather . . . and now a new baby in the family."

"I'm excited about the baby," Mei insisted. "And Stan is . . . okay."

They exchanged glances and giggled. "Truly," Mei said, now feeling protective of Stan, of all people, "Stan and I are getting along fine. You don't have to worry about me, Mom."

"Moms always worry, honey. And even when I seem wrapped up in the baby, I always have one set of brain cells focused exclusively on you."

"Yuck, Mom. I thought Dad was the scientist in the family."

Her mom pulled a wisp of stray hair out of her face, then relaxed back onto her palms. "You're so much like your dad," she said. "True, you get your artistic genius from me"—she laughed lightly—"but you've got your father's disposition: quiet on the outside, but always observing, always noticing every little thing. A real thinker."

"So Dad was a geek, too?" Mei teased.

Her mom's eyes danced. "I remember the first time I met him. He was walking out of a classroom with his head buried in a book. He walked right into me."

Mei sat up straight and squeezed her knees toward her chest. "Did he ask you out right away?"

Her mother chuckled. "If you consider a year later right away. He was so shy. I practically had to shove my phone number under his nose. And of course, I kept 'accidentally' turning up in places I knew he'd be."

Mei's brow furrowed. "So all that stuff really works? You know . . . 'accidentally' showing up where you know some guy will be?"

Her mom looked intrigued. "Sounds like you've got some specific guy on your mind."

"No, no!" Mei protested, covering her face with her hands.

"It's okay, honey. It's not a crime to have a crush, you know."

"No crushes!" Mei moaned through her hands.

Her mom leaned in with a twinkle in her eyes. "So: Is he cute?"

Mei giggled and lowered her hands. She was busted. "Not particularly," she said coyly. "But he's really smart."

"And? Does he like you, too?"

Mei blushed. "He barely knows I exist. I can't even bring myself to say hi to him."

"You and your dad: two peas in a pod."

A wistful look crossed Mei's face. Yes. She really was like her father.

"I'm too young for a boyfriend anyhow," she said.

"Well, I can't help agreeing with that. But it never hurts to make new friends. He's smart, you're smart. . . . Look at what he's reading next time you see him, and make some astute observation to get a conversation going. Or sit next to him in class and borrow a pencil."

"Mother. That's so retro."

"I'm just thinking of icebreakers, that's all." Mei's mother leaned forward and clasped her daughter's hand. "And that's all it'll take, sweetie: breaking the ice. You're a wonderful girl–smart, funny, caring. Once you move past your shyness, it'll be easy for guys to see all your wonderful qualities. And remember: friendship. That's all you need at this age, and that's the source of any great romance."

"Ah, romance," Mei cooed, then crossed her eyes and stuck her tongue out the side of her mouth.

"My little beauty," her mother teased, wrapping her arms around her daughter. They plopped to the floor together, laughing.

15

Tricia hadn't even had a chance to call the next Right-Under Club meeting to order when Leighton strode purposefully over to the Problem Stick and held it aloft.

"My turn," she announced tersely.

Tricia, Mei and Hope exchanged amused glances. They had giggled among themselves the past couple of weeks, speculating about what problem Leighton might share when it was her turn to hold the Problem Stick. A broken nail? A sudden spike in humidity making her hair frizz? With a life as complicated as Leighton's, the possibilities were endless.

"What are you all looking at?" Leighton asked suspiciously, noticing their furtive glances.

"Nothing," Tricia said quickly. "Elizabeth's not back yet from her grandparents' to report on old business, so I make a motion that we go straight to new business and listen to Leighton's problem. Do I hear a second?"

"Second," Mei said.

"All in favor?"

The girls all raised their hands.

"Leighton," Tricia said. "Let's hear your problem."

Hope sucked in her lips to camouflage her grin.

Leighton shifted her weight and put a hand on her hip. "I've got a big problem," she announced in a lowered voice. "A big problem."

"Oooh," Hope said under her breath, then burst into sputtered giggles with Mei.

"Order," Tricia said sternly. "Leighton has the floor."

Leighton shot an icy glance at Hope and Mei, then tightened her grip on the Problem Stick.

"My cousin's getting married July tenth," she continued. "I don't even like her, so I figured I could get out of it easily enough. But my mom is insisting that I go." She *hmmph*ed indignantly.

"What's the big deal?" Tricia asked.

"The big deal," Leighton said evenly, as if it should be obvious, "is that my whole family has to go. And since my mom has ruined my life by adding Clueless Kyle Clayton to the family, that means he has to go, too."

She paused for dramatic effect so the gravity of her situation could sink in.

Hope gave an exaggerated yawn. "So his cooties rub off if you're in the same room?" she asked.

Leighton glared at her. "For your information, there are going to be lots of cool people at the wedding, including a certain high school hottie I've been crushing on for months. Does the name Scott ring a bell?"

"You're too young for high school guys," Mei said.

"Oh, thanks, Mommy," Leighton snarled. "True, Scott is totally hot, and true, he sends me flirty instant messages every single day, and true, everyone knows we'd make the most awesome couple ever, but Mei's right: I should spend all my time playing hopscotch."

She tossed her brown hair over her shoulder. "You girls are so immature."

"How do you even know a high school guy?" Tricia asked.

"He saw my Web page and sent me an IM saying we should hook up."

Tricia cringed. "Hook up," she repeated. "Leighton, do you know what that means?"

"Uh, duh!" Leighton responded. "It means he wants to be my boyfriend."

"Are you sure?" Tricia persisted. "I have some cousins in high school, and . . ."

Leighton tossed her hands in the air in exasperation. "Would you chill? Just because you guys are clueless about high school boys doesn't mean I am. You are so unsophisticated. I'm, like, ten times more mature than all of you put together."

"Scott is too old for you," Hope said evenly. "And if we're so immature, why are you hanging out with us?"

Leighton narrowed her ocean green eyes. "When will you be old enough for a boyfriend, Hope? When you're thirty?"

Hope blushed and stared at her lap.

"Girls! Focus," Tricia barked. "We're a club, remember? We're supposed to support each other. And we aren't here to judge. We're here to help."

Leighton sneered at Hope. "And it just so happens that I have totally gone out of my way to try to help Kyle."

Hope snickered.

"I give him pointers on how to dress, and how to fix his hair, and how to stop using big words that nobody understands," Leighton continued. "So I've tried. But he refuses to take my advice, and I refuse to let my reputation go right down the drain because of him."

"Yeah, you'd hate for people to think you approved of using big words," Hope said. "Like 'superficial,' maybe. Or 'arrogant.' "

"What are you talking about?" Leighton demanded, and Hope sucked in her cheeks again to squelch a grin.

"Hey, I helped you with your little spa day problem," Leighton reminded her.

"Leighton's right," Tricia said. "Whatever her problem is, it's our mission as Right-Unders to try to help her solve it. So think 'helpful.' " She shot a disapproving look at Hope, who flung her hands in the air in surrender.

"Fine," Hope said. "Helpful."

"This wedding is going to be a nightmare," Leighton continued. "A band will play at the reception, and I just know Kyle's going to humiliate me by dancing."

Hope held her tongue.

"There he'll be," Leighton said, "flapping his arms like a chicken on the dance floor, probably with his fly open. I'll die. I'll just die."

She handed the Problem Stick to Tricia. "That's my problem."

Tricia propped the stick against the cedar wall of the tree house. "Girls, you've heard Leighton's problem," she said. "Now it's time to come up with solutions. Your five minutes starts"—she glanced at her watch—"now."

Tricia, Hope and Mei opened their notebooks and started writing. Hope wasted no time. "GET OVER YOURSELF," she penciled in bold letters, then sighed and flipped to a blank page.

As a Right-Under, she was supposed to take her responsibility seriously. But how could anyone take Leighton seriously? She was off-the-charts obnoxious. Nothing would help her more than being brought down a peg or two. Actually, that would be a service to humanity in general. But, particularly with Elizabeth absent from the meeting and with only three solutions in the bowl, she didn't want her answer to stand out like a sore thumb. Helpful, she thought grumpily. Helpful.

Mei didn't know where to begin with her blank sheet of paper. It was a problem to be with Kyle? Sign her up for that problem. Why did she have to be so shy? Her mother was right. She needed to loosen up a little. Why couldn't she just walk up to Kyle and start a conversation? Maybe he'd notice her mural. . . .

"Time's up!" Tricia announced.

"Oh, give me just one more minute," Mei pleaded.

Tricia nodded. "One more minute."

Mei finally scribbled something on her paper.

"Time's up," Tricia said a minute later. The girls folded their papers twice and placed them in the Solutions Bowl.

"Mei's turn this time," Hope said. Mei shrugged with a smile and took the bowl.

"Here goes," she said, unfolding the papers. She read them aloud:

"SOLUTION: Don't mind what other people think about Kyle. Try to have a good time at the wedding and don't get embarrassed by him just because he's having fun. Remember: the people who mind don't matter and the people who matter don't mind.

"SOLUTION: Go buy some new stilettos—as if you need any more—and step on Kyle's toe so he'll be in too much pain to dance!

"SOLUTION: When the dancing starts, get a 'headache' and make your mom take you home."

Leighton rolled her eyes. "Like, what I need is to get out of going to the wedding altogether," she groused.

"But we deal in practicalities," Tricia said. "Your mom's going to make you go, so make the best of it . . . hopefully without putting Kyle in traction."

• • •

BOOM!

Tricia's sister, Everly, covered her ears and screeched, half playfully, half fearfully.

"They're just fireworks, silly," Tricia said, holding her sister tighter.

"Look, Everly," Mei said, pointing skyward as more bright colors exploded overhead. "Aren't they pretty?"

"Too loud," Everly assessed, but she was obviously having a good time. Tricia's mom and stepdad had suggested that Tricia invite her friends to the city's Fourth of July fireworks display, and they were all snuggling on the riverbank in the cool night air. They were surrounded by hundreds of people, but the blanket felt cozy and intimate.

"A blue one!" Everly said, bouncing on her big sister's lap.

"Be still, Hissy," Tricia said.

"Don't call your sister Hissy," her mother said in the monotone she reserved for if-I've-told-you-once-I've-told-you-a-thousand-times commands. Tricia teasingly hissed in her sister's ear. Everly squealed on cue.

"How's Elizabeth doing at her grandparents' house?" Tricia asked Hope.

"Okay, I guess. She called yesterday and didn't sound too desperate. She said she'd give us the 411 when she gets back. She loved that we went to see her. She couldn't stop talking about it."

"Good," Tricia said. "How about Jacie? Is she still driving you crazy?"

"Oh, she's my BFF," Hope cooed sarcastically.

Mei frowned. "I thought you two were getting along better."

Tricia smiled knowingly. "Even if they were, Hope would never admit it," she said. "It's easier for Hope to make jokes than to get real. Too bad for Jacie that she's the butt of the jokes."

Tricia's tone was light, but Hope felt a pang of irritation. Maybe if Tricia's mom hit the road and never looked back, Tricia would be reluctant to "get real," too. Maybe reality was highly overrated.

But she shook off her annoyance. Fireworks lit the sky. She was with friends. She shifted to default mode: humor. "Hey, why don't we start a Jacie fan club?" she said. "But instead of pink T-shirts, let's go with black for this club. Slimming, you know."

"Sounds right up Leighton's alley," Tricia said.

"Hey . . . speaking of Leighton . . . what's she doing tonight?" Mei asked.

"I dunno," Tricia said, then felt a twinge of guilt. "I guess I should've invited her to come with us tonight. But fireworks with the family . . . it doesn't seem like her style."

"Yeah, the fireworks migh leave her hair smelling sooty," Hope said, rolling her eyes. "We couldn't have Miss Perfect smelling of smoke, now could we?"

The girls giggled, but again exchanged anxious glances. It didn't feel right to be making fun of fellow Right-Unders, even if Leighton practically begged to be made fun of.

"She's not so bad," Tricia said protectively.

"Wait till school starts," Hope said. "She'll treat you like you have the plague. She's got a reputation to protect, you know. She's bored enough this summer to tolerate us, but once cheerleading season begins, it'll be a whole new story."

"An old story, actually," Mei added wryly.

Still . . . Tricia wished she'd at least asked Leighton if she wanted to come to the fireworks show. It felt like the least she could do for a fellow Right-Under.

• • •

BOOM!

Elizabeth's grandmother smiled nervously. "They're so loud."

Elizabeth and her grandfather looked at each other. They hadn't been sure whether the fireworks show at the lake would be a good idea. Even after the short time Elizabeth had spent with her grandparents, she could tell her grandmother was becoming increasingly moody and unpredictable.

"We don't have to go," Elizabeth had told her grandfather earlier in the day, sensing he was making the effort for her sake.

"We need to go," her grandfather responded, nodding sharply. "If it doesn't go well, we can always leave."

So there they were, sitting on lawn chairs on the shore of the lake, surrounded by dozens of other onlookers. Elizabeth was enjoying the chirps of crickets and the croaks of frogs as much as she was enjoying the fireworks. She felt invigorated in the evening air under the starlit sky. And tomorrow, she was going back to Hope's house.

She smiled at the thought, then swallowed hard to push down a lump in her throat. How could she be happy about leaving? Her visit had been tough, but it had also been kind of . . . special. As more pages were added to the scrapbook every day, Elizabeth had learned more and more about her grandmother. She'd learned how her grandma had broken her arm in fourth grade falling off a jungle gym, and how she had adopted a motherless squirrel one summer, and how she had baked her first brown Betty one rainy Sunday afternoon for a boy she had a crush on. What Elizabeth had learned most of all was that her grandmother needed her now. It felt good to be there for her.

Her grandma's face softened in the glow of the glittery night sky. She was smiling, sometimes even clapping in delight. The moment might not last; she might turn angry or fearful any second now. Elizabeth pushed every unpleasant thought from her mind and intertwined her fingers with her grandma's. At this moment, her grandmother was happy. And that was enough.

16

Elizabeth flew into Hope's arms the next day as Hope got out of the car in the Carsons' dusty driveway.

"I missed you," Elizabeth said, resisting the urge to cry.

"We missed you, too," Hope said, feeling her cousin's heart pound against her chest as they held each other tightly. "You'll have to tell me all about your visit on the ride home."

Elizabeth pulled away and shook her head. "Can we wait a couple of days? Until the next Right-Under meeting?"

Hope wrinkled her brow. "Sure," she said. "I just thought you'd be full of stories after ten days on the farm."

Elizabeth's eyes fell.

"Elizabeth?" Hope probed anxiously. "What's wrong?

"Nothing. I just . . . I just want to go home and act goofy for a few days."

Hope's dad walked around the car and tousled Elizabeth's hair. "We missed you, squirt!" he said.

She hugged him.

"Hello, Jack," her grandpa said, coming down the driveway and extending his hand. "The missus isn't feeling so well. She said to tell you hello."

"Well, please give her my best," Hope's dad said. "Elizabeth, did you say goodbye to your grandmother?"

A light breeze blew through Elizabeth's blond curls. "Yes," she said. She turned to hug her grandfather. "I'll see you soon," she whispered in his ear.

He held her tighter. As she pulled away, she saw that his eyes were moist with tears.

"Grandpa?"

She was ready to march right back inside with her suitcases if he wanted her to. All he had to do was say the word. He smiled warmly, seeming to read her mind.

"We'll be fine," he said firmly.

Hope's dad cleared his throat. "We better hit the road," he said, taking a suitcase in each hand.

Elizabeth kissed her grandpa's cheek. "I'll call tonight, after Mom gets here," she said. A silly thought crossed her mind: Since Elizabeth was "Margaret" to her grandma most of the time now, who would Margaret be? "Take good care of Grandma," she said to her grandfather.

"Take good care of yourself," he told her. She got in the car and waved as it pulled away, leaving her grandpa in their dusty trail.

• • •

"The July eighth meeting of the Right-Under Club is now in session."

Tricia tapped the Problem Stick on the floor like a gavel, then looked from one member's face to the next.

"Welcome back, Elizabeth," she said. "We had a blast on

the farm, by the way." Elizabeth waved with a bashful smile. "Leighton, since your cousin's wedding isn't until Saturday, we'll follow up on your problem next week. Today, we'll follow up on Elizabeth's. Elizabeth, how was your visit with your grandparents?"

Elizabeth paused and stared at her hands, trying to decide what to say. But when she raised her eyes and began talking, her voice was surprisingly firm.

"My grandmother has Alzheimer's disease," she said.

An uneasy silence hung in the air.

"Is that the old-people disease where you lose your mind?" Leighton finally asked. The girls tossed her withering glances. "Okay, chill," Leighton responded. "I was just asking."

"Alzheimer's means you start forgetting things," Elizabeth explained patiently.

"Why?" Leighton persisted. The other girls looked uncomfortable, but Elizabeth didn't seem to mind talking about it.

"I've been reading about it on the Internet," she said. "Doctors don't really know what causes it, but this stuff called plaque starts building up in your brain."

"Like the gunk on your teeth?" Leighton said.

Elizabeth shrugged. "I'm not really sure. But whatever it is, it sort of short-circuits your memory. Especially recent stuff. It's funny . . . Grandma remembers songs from when she was a kid, but she has trouble remembering whether she's eaten breakfast."

"My aunt had Alzheimer's disease," Mei said. "She didn't even know her own name. Shouldn't your grandmother be in a nursing home?"

Elizabeth's lips tightened. "Maybe. Grandma's sister had it, and that's where she ended up. But she was in really bad shape.

Grandma's memory kind of comes and goes. Sometimes, you wouldn't know anything was wrong with her. But not most of the time. I told my grandpa I didn't think it was safe for her to be alone. He got a little mad at first, but he knows I'm right. We had a long talk with my mom. She's spending some time with them now, and she and Grandpa will decide what they need to do next."

Hope's eyes searched Elizabeth's. "Why didn't you say something?" she asked. "You were there for over a week. You should've called us right away. I could have helped you."

"It was okay," Elizabeth responded. "Grandpa and I turned into a pretty good team. I got better at understanding how to help Grandma. I liked being able to help her." She folded her hands in her lap. "We made a scrapbook."

"A scrapbook?" Tricia said.

Elizabeth nodded. "I didn't want to leave her alone, and there wasn't much to do. So I thought a scrapbook might be fun . . . that it might help her, you know? Grandma has dozens of old pictures, and I brought my digital camera, so I took lots more. I thought pictures might help her remember. Pictures of people, pets, stuff around the house . . . that kind of thing."

"That was a really good idea," Tricia said quietly.

"I think so, too," Elizabeth said. "She keeps it on her coffee table. She likes looking through it just for fun, and sometimes she really needs it. She was trying to explain something to Grandpa the other day and got really confused. She started flipping through the scrapbook and saw the picture of the toaster. I wrote the name of it and what you use it for by the picture. She was so glad to see that picture. She said, 'Toaster! That's the word I was looking for!' "

Elizabeth smiled at the memory.

"Wow," Leighton said, shaking her head slowly. "I would've freaked if it had been me."

"I was kinda scared at first," Elizabeth conceded. "And I was really sad. But after the shock wore off, it wasn't so bad."

"Does your grandma know who you are?" Mei asked.

"Sometimes. Other times she calls me Margaret, my mom's name. And a few times, she looked at me like she'd never seen me before in her life. Creepy, huh? So I've been asking her a million questions about her life while I still have a chance. You know what it's like when somebody breaks open a piñata and you scramble to collect all the candy that's falling out? I felt like I was scrambling to collect all Grandma's memories before they fell out."

Hope's eyes glistened with tears. "But I wish you'd let us help you," she said.

Elizabeth peered at a ray of sunlight streaming in through a slit in the cedar planks of the tree house. "It's okay," she said. "It was time for me to do the helping."

• • •

None of them could put the feeling into words, but the Right-Unders were anxious for a change of scenery after hearing Elizabeth's story. It was time to step out of the box of the tree house and do something different. Tricia even postponed the new business of turning over the Problem Stick to someone else. A new problem would have to wait for next Thursday's meeting. For now . . .

"Ice cream!" Tricia announced. "Let's make sundaes."

The girls left the tree house one by one, crouching out the door and inching gingerly down the spiral steps. The backyard smelled of honeysuckle and jasmine. The girls drank in the scent. They carried their flip-flops in their hands so they could sink their toes into the thick grass in Tricia's yard. Tricia led them to the deck that extended from the back of her house.

"Sit at the patio table and I'll bring the ice cream out here," Tricia said. She went inside through the back door, then came back out a few minutes later with four kinds of ice cream tucked in her arms. Her mom came behind her carrying bowls, followed by Everly, who gleefully tumbled headlong into her sister's legs.

"Ice cream!" Everly sang.

"So do you girls have a club or something?" Tricia's mom asked as she scooped ice cream into the bowls. "Tricia refuses to tell me what R.U. stands for."

The girls giggled conspiratorially.

"We could tell you, but then we'd have to kill you," Tricia deadpanned.

"Then I'll have to guess," her mom said. "Red umbrella? Ripped underwear? Rich uncle?"

The girls laughed. "Not even close," Tricia said. "Give it up, Mom."

Her mom handed out the bowls. "Aren't you glad Troy made you that tree house?" she asked Tricia.

"I thought it was Everly's tree house," Hope said.

Tricia blushed, recalling how embarrassed she'd been when her new friends spotted the tree house . . . how babyish she'd thought it would seem, how she'd pawned it off as Everly's.

"Your stepdad made it for you?" Leighton asked.

Tricia shrugged noncommittally.

"What a great stepdad," Mei said.

I wouldn't go that far, Tricia thought.

"He made it himself? With his very own hands?" Elizabeth said.

Tricia nodded. What was the big deal?

"Wow," Elizabeth said. "He just may be the coolest stepdad on the planet."

"Certainly cooler than mine," Leighton said.

Tricia's mom brushed her index finger against her daughter's nose. " 'Cool' is not the word Tricia usually uses to describe her stepfather," she told the others, but her tone was playful.

"He's okay," Tricia said grudgingly.

"Just okay?" Mei asked.

Just okay, Tricia thought to herself. She knew it wasn't fair, but it didn't really matter how cool Troy was. It wasn't who he was that was the problem. It was who he wasn't.

17

"Leighton Lockwood. Let's go! *Now!*"

Leighton rolled her eyes. Why was her mother always rushing her? That woman spent half her life standing at the foot of the stairs hollering for her daughter to hurry up. Didn't she realize that beauty can't be rushed?

Leighton carefully applied blush to the apples of her cheeks. She still had to straighten her hair, which would take another ten minutes. Her mom could just chill. If they were a few minutes late, well, it served her mom right for making Leighton go to this stupid wedding in the first place. Besides, she had to look just right for Scott. Perfection took time.

Kyle poked his head into her bedroom. "Why do you have to stress her out every time we go somewhere?" he asked his stepsister.

Leighton tossed him a sidelong look. Half his shirttail was hanging out of his pants, and his tie was too short. His glasses were askew and his hair was tousled. He was hopeless.

"Out!" Leighton snapped, but Kyle lingered.

"It's really inconsiderate to keep everybody waiting," he said.

Leighton snapped her blush container shut. "If I was

content to look like you," she said with a sneer, "I could be ready in five minutes flat. But if little things like combed hair and basic hygiene are priorities, you'll need to give me a few extra seconds."

Kyle shook his head. "You drive your mother crazy," he said. "And she's such a nice person."

"Do you mind? I don't need you to tell me about my mother."

The nerve. Had Leighton asked to share her life with two strangers? Had she asked her dad to split and never look back when she was only two? Not that it bothered her . . . she wasn't like some whiny kids who blamed every problem on an absentee dad. Leighton never even missed the guy. Who needed him? She had her mom. They were best friends; they did everything together. Until Kyle's dad had arrived on the scene, that is, bringing Klunky Kyle along for the ride. And now Kyle had the nerve to stand in her bedroom doorway telling her what her mom was like. Please.

"Go away, Kyle. The musty smell of your suit is wilting my hair."

Leighton grasped the heated hair straightener and pulled it through her chestnut locks.

Kyle shrugged and walked out of the room.

That was another thing Leighton hated about Kyle. He never stood up for himself. Sometimes, Leighton intentionally goaded him just to get a rise out of him. She was doing him a favor, really. Did he want to be a wimp forever?

But her efforts were futile. Kyle never took the bait. The nastier she got, the faster he retreated. Hopeless.

By this time, Leighton's mom was bellowing up the stairs. "*Let's go!*"

"God!" Leighton said, unplugging the hair straightener. "Have a heart attack, why don't you?"

She spun on a stiletto heel (she knew the suggestion was Hope's, but it wasn't half bad) and strode downstairs.

"You," her mother said with bulging eyes, "are impossible."

"Can we just get this over with?" Leighton muttered. She headed for the front door, followed by her mom, her stepdad and Kyle.

She hated riding in a car with Kyle. He had no concept of personal space. His long legs were constantly creeping over to her half of the backseat. Even worse, he was always fidgeting. He'd get some song stuck in his head, then start singing softly to himself, at which point the fingertips would start tapping. Sometimes he'd drum on his thighs; then the legs would start pumping to the beat. Before she knew it, his leg would be flapping like a chicken wing into her space.

"Get *off* me!" she snarled, swatting at his wayward leg.

He moved his leg, but she knew it was only a matter of time before the cycle repeated itself.

"Can't you drive any faster?" she whined to her stepfather, who tossed his head noncommittally. Mr. Motor Mouth, that was Carl. If he uttered more than five words a day, it was cause to alert the media. What did her mom see in that guy? And once she had realized Kyle was part of the package, what had kept her from fleeing in the opposite direction?

Her mom used to be so fun, always brushing Leighton's hair and organizing sleepovers, complete with homemade cookies and silly makeup sessions. Leighton didn't get invited to other girls' homes very often—not that she cared—so the sleepovers gave her a chance to hang out and have fun. It was weird . . . everyone wanted to be like her, but they didn't particularly want to be with her, except in the school lunchroom, where they tripped over each other trying to sit next to her so they could score popularity points. As for true friendships . . . well, the kids were just too jealous of Leighton to really get close to her. Even Catastrophe Kyle had a few good friends. Sure, their nerd quotient was off the charts, but Leighton couldn't help feeling a pang of envy.

She stared out the window as tidy little front yards blurred into a single sea of green. Without her mom as a best friend anymore, Leighton couldn't deny her loneliness. Except that now she had the Right-Under Club. They were her friends . . . right?

• • •

Leighton propped her elbow on the table and sank her chin into the palm of her hand. The wedding ceremony was over, and now the part she dreaded was here: the reception. Round tables with starchy white tablecloths dotted the room. Buffet tables were lined against a wall; Leighton cringed as she spotted her stepfather filling his plate with meatballs. A band played on a platform at the other end of the room, and couples were starting to dance. Scott kept stealing glances at her from a couple of tables over. She sipped a diet soda, tossing occasional sidelong glances in his direction. If he wanted to dance, he'd have to come to her. She was playing it cool.

"Wanna dance?"

Oh, God. Kyle was suddenly standing beside her chair, extending a hand.

Not in this lifetime.

"You can dance?" Leighton asked Kyle.

He blushed. "I can try."

"Try with my grandmother," Leighton suggested, then turned her back and took another sip of soda. Kyle slinked away. Wimp.

"Leighton!" her mom whispered from the seat beside her. "I will not have you being rude to Kyle!"

Leighton's jaw dropped. "I'm not going to pulverize my reputation by dancing with him," she spat in an angry whisper.

"He is your stepbrother and he is a perfectly darling young man," her mother said sharply. "You should be proud to be his stepsister."

Right.

Luckily, Kyle had taken Leighton up on her suggestion and asked her grandmother for a dance. There they were . . . her grandmother, beaming from ear to ear, and gawky Kyle, flapping his arms and clomping around the dance floor in his impossibly clunky shoes. Oh, brother . . .

"You need a serious attitude adjustment, young lady," Leighton's mother said through gritted teeth.

Leighton managed a nonchalant look, but her heart sank. When had her mother started hating her? She felt a thud in her stomach.

"Would you like to dance?"

Leighton glanced up, startled. There he was: Scott. Her heart skipped a beat. She paused for a moment, flustered. A few extra couples had joined the dance floor, so maybe Kyle wasn't too noticeable right now. Maybe Scott wouldn't know they were related.

"Okay," she said casually, rising as Scott took her hand.

She registered her mom's look of concern as she brushed past her. Moms.

Just as Scott and Leighton reached the dance floor, the band started a slow song. Leighton laced her fingers behind Scott's neck as he supported the small of her back, caressing the fabric of her ankle-length satin dress, which matched her green eyes. She tried to look bored as they swayed back and forth, but every once in a while, her eyes would fall on Scott . . . his dirty blond hair, his blue eyes, his firm chin. Ooooh, he was cute!

"So what are you doing for fun this summer?" Scott asked her.

She shrugged. "Just chilling."

"Me too." He subtly pulled her close. "We should chill together."

Leighton's heartbeat quickened. "That could be arranged."

Scott grinned. "Your mom would let you hang out with me? You're . . . what . . . still in middle school?"

Leighton tossed her hair out of her face. "I'm almost fourteen."

Scott's grin broadened. "Yeah . . . you're definitely getting older. So your mom really would let you go out with me?"

"Duh." Except that she probably wouldn't. Which meant that Leighton might have to be a little . . . creative when she told her mom where she was going. As if her mom cared anyway.

Leighton smiled at Scott, then purred, "I think I could arrange to squeeze you into my schedule."

Scott's eyelids lowered. "How about now?" he asked in a low, breathy voice.

A flash of confusion crossed Leighton's face, but she quickly masked it. "Now?"

"Yeah. Now. I got a new car. It's right outside in the parking lot. We can duck out for a few minutes and nobody will even know we're missing." He paused. "What do you say?"

Leighton swallowed hard. Why was her stomach hurting? This was just what she wanted . . . right? She had fantasized for months about being with Scott. But once she was with him, what would they do? She hadn't thought that far ahead, and the prospect made her palms sweaty. Still, this was her chance. No way would she blow it.

"Sure," she said coolly.

Scott held a finger of her hand and guided her from the dance floor. Leighton glanced anxiously at her mother, who was still sitting at the table but was now talking animatedly to other guests. Her mom would seriously freak if she realized Leighton was missing, but she'd be back in just a few minutes. Scott was right. No one would even know they were gone. What was the big deal?

Leighton took a deep breath. Maybe Scott would kiss her. She pushed past her anxiety to enjoy the moment. This was perfect.

He led her from the reception hall, through the foyer and to the front door. As he reached for the doorknob, Leighton suddenly pulled back.

"Uh . . . why don't we just hang out here for a few minutes? It's kinda muggy outside. Humidity does a real number on my hair."

How lame! Why was she acting like a ten-year-old? What was the big deal about going into the parking lot to see his new car? Now he'd know for sure that she was hopelessly immature. Still, she couldn't quite make herself follow him outside.

"C'mon," Scott coaxed. "Don't you want to see my wheels?"

"What kind of car is it?" she asked, stalling for time.

"A Jaguar. Vintage."

"I thought you drove a Camaro," she said.

"Wrecked it," Scott replied matter-of-factly. "My dad bought me this one last week. So come on outside. I'll show it to you."

The drumbeat from the band seemed to be mimicking the pounding in Leighton's chest. "I told you, it's muggy outside." She cocked her head to one side and smiled coyly. "We've got plenty of privacy right here, don't you think?"

Scott scrutinized her for a moment, then narrowed his eyes. "Whatever."

The next moment came so quickly that Leighton didn't have time to react. Scott grabbed her forearms roughly and pulled her against his chest. His face pressed against hers; then his mouth seemed to swallow hers whole.

Leighton instinctively drew back, but his hand held her face firmly in place. This was what kissing felt like? She had imagined it would be tender and romantic. Why was Scott being so rough? He was pushing so hard against her lips that she was struggling to breathe. His whiskers were scratching her cheeks.

"I can't breathe!" The words were trapped in her mind. She wanted to push Scott away, but he was effortlessly holding her still. He was at least five inches taller and probably eighty pounds heavier that she was. She felt like a rag doll in his arms. This wasn't what kissing was supposed to feel like. This wasn't how a boyfriend was supposed to act. She wondered if she should bite him, just to regain some control. That was it. . . . She would bite him. . . .

"Get your paws off my sister, jerk."

Scott pulled away from Leighton so abruptly that her head snapped back sharply. They turned simultaneously toward the sound of the voice.

"Kyle . . . ," Leighton said, gasping for air.

"Lighten up, man," Scott snarled at him, shaking the stiffness out of his shoulders.

"You stay away from her." Kyle's voice was so steely, so menacing. Leighton had never heard him sound like that before.

"No prob, little guy," Scott spat, then tightened his tie brusquely, cut his eyes at Leighton and muttered, "You're way too young for me anyway. Next time, find yourself a pimple-faced little eighth grader to tease."

He strode from the foyer back into the reception hall.

Leighton backed into the wall of the foyer and crumpled to the floor like a candy wrapper. She lowered her head and wept.

Kyle knelt beside her and stroked her hair. "It's okay," he murmured.

"Stupid, stupid, stupid!" Leighton sputtered, wiping her eyes roughly with the backs of her hands. "I am so stupid!"

"No," Kyle said gently. "Scott is a moron. It wasn't you. It was him."

Leighton's ocean-colored eyes glittered through her tears as she stared earnestly at her stepbrother. "I thought he was a nice guy." She laughed bitterly. "I thought he wanted to be my boyfriend."

"It's okay," Kyle repeated. "It's okay."

He lowered himself to the floor and sat by her side, putting an arm around her and holding her close.

"These things happen," Kyle said. "Guys are jerks."

Leighton's eyes locked with his. "Not you," she said.

Kyle managed a weak smile. "I hope not."

Leighton grasped his hand. "Kyle," she said in a voice that was suddenly firm. "Thank you."

He shrugged. "Anytime."

She wrapped her arms around his neck and hugged him tightly. He hugged her back.

18

"Can you call an emergency Right-Under meeting?"

Leighton's voice on the phone was so shaky that Tricia didn't hesitate. "Yes," she said decisively. "Come right over. I'll call the other girls now."

Tricia's phone call interrupted Hope's and Elizabeth's Sunday lunch, but her tone conveyed urgency. "We'll be right over," they said.

Mei was in her basement painting when Tricia called. She'd be there in five minutes, she said.

Tricia rushed outside, hurried up the steps to the tree house, crouched through the door, then held the Problem Stick and sat down with her knees to her chest. Leighton had sounded so upset. What could be wrong? Had Kyle embarrassed her at the wedding the night before? No . . . it sounded more serious than that.

Hope and Elizabeth arrived first, then Leighton, who sat in a corner of the tree house, gazing at the floor silently. After Mei arrived, Tricia tapped the Problem Stick against the floor.

"This emergency meeting of the Right-Under Club is now in session," she said solemnly.

All eyes fell on Leighton, who was hugging her knees to her chest and rocking slowly back and forth.

"What's up?" Tricia asked her softly.

Tears welled in Leighton's eyes, then flowed freely down her cheeks. The girls exchanged anxious glances. Leighton crying? She was always so cool, so self-assured. What could possibly be wrong?

They were silent for a couple of moments as Leighton sniffled and wiped tears from her eyes.

"Did . . . something happen . . . at your cousin's wedding?" Elizabeth asked haltingly.

Leighton nodded, then cried some more.

"Was it Kyle?" Hope asked.

Leighton rubbed her eyes and looked at the girls evenly. "I'm such an idiot," she said.

"Tell us," Tricia prodded.

Leighton took a deep breath. "We went to the wedding last night," she said, staring straight ahead at the wall of the tree house. "Scott—the guy from high school?—asked me to dance during the reception."

The girls leaned in closer.

"He asked me if I wanted to go outside and see his new car."

Tricia drew in a quick breath.

"We got to the foyer and I decided I shouldn't go any further. So he started kissing me right there. Only it didn't feel like kissing. He was pinning his mouth against mine and kind of . . . kind of mauling me. I couldn't get away. It was awful."

The girls huddled around her. Elizabeth put her hand on Leighton's knee. Tricia rubbed her back.

"Did he hurt you?" Elizabeth whispered.

Leighton shook her head vigorously. "Kyle came and stopped him."

The girls' relief was audible. Finally, they felt as if they could breathe again.

"Wow," Mei murmured. "I always knew Kyle was a great guy."

Leighton's eyes fell. "I didn't. I'm such an idiot. I thought Scott was a great guy. By the end of the night, I saw him kissing another girl on the dance floor."

"Leighton, you have to be careful," Hope said, surprising everyone with the urgency in her tone. "You have to watch out for yourself. I hear guys talking about you, and you . . . you . . . well, you just have to be careful, that's all."

Leighton started crying again.

"Oh, Leighton . . . I didn't mean to make you cry," Hope said.

"No," she responded. "It's okay. You're right." She looked steadily at the girls through her tears. "We all have to be careful."

They nodded, but Elizabeth looked troubled. "I don't want to go around being afraid of guys all the time. Are all guys that way?"

"Just some," Hope clarified.

"Yeah," Mei said. "Look at Kyle. He's a great guy."

"But let's make a Right-Under pledge right now," Tricia said. "Make sure you really know a guy . . . and really trust him . . . before you're alone with him."

"It's important," Leighton emphasized. "You think you'll be able to handle a situation, but you might be totally kidding yourself. I couldn't do anything to help myself. Scott had me pinned against him. I could barely even move. I don't know what I would've done if Kyle hadn't come along."

"I'm sorry that happened to you," Elizabeth said.

Leighton's tightened lips slipped into a weak smile. "Thanks. And thanks for listening."

"You don't have to thank us for that," Tricia said. "We're Right-Unders, remember? We R There for U."

Leighton hugged her knees tighter against her chest. "Yeah . . . but sometimes I still feel like an outsider . . . you know?"

"What do you mean?" Tricia asked nervously.

Leighton glanced from one Right-Under to the next. "The way you guys make fun of me. Every time I come into the clubhouse, you all get quiet. I know you're talking about me."

The girls' eyes fell.

"And the way you get together and do things without inviting me," Leighton continued.

"I didn't think you'd like fireworks!" Tricia said defensively.

Leighton's eyes softened. "It's okay," she said. "I don't blame you. I know I can be snotty. And you're here for me now. That really means a lot."

Hope's brow knitted as she searched for the right words. "We are your friends," she said slowly. "But you kinda push people away . . . the way you're always judging us . . . looking down on us and making us feel bad."

Leighton met Hope's eyes. "I'm sorry," she said sincerely. "I feel judged a lot, too. Like I'm just not fitting in."

"But you fit in everywhere," Hope responded. "Everybody wants to be just like you."

Leighton shook her head. "But people don't really like me. I thought about telling you guys when it was my turn with the Problem Stick. But how do you complain to people who don't like you that nobody likes you?"

The girls managed nervous chuckles.

"We like you," Elizabeth said.

Leighton lowered her eyes and shook her head. "Even my mom doesn't like me. She used to be my best friend, and now . . ."

"Now what?" Tricia asked.

Leighton shrugged. "She just acts . . . annoyed with me a lot. Big surprise, huh?"

The girls felt the tension dissipate as they allowed themselves to laugh freely.

"But as horrible as last night was, my mom was so there for me. When we got home, I told her what happened with Scott and she just . . . held me."

Hope looked wistful. "I wish I had a mom like that. My mom didn't even remember my birthday."

Elizabeth touched her cousin's leg. "But you have a great dad," she said.

Hope nodded. "I know. But I envy you guys. I'd give my right arm to have any one of your moms."

The girls averted their eyes.

"Hey," Tricia said. "We've got each other, right? And no more gossiping about each other or making snide remarks. We may feel like leftovers in our families sometimes, but we'll always be Right-Unders to each other."

Tricia held her arms out by her sides, then folded them around her friends. They all followed her lead, one after the other. There they sat . . . the Right-Unders, a single solid circle.

• • •

She'd only known them a few weeks, but Tricia was realizing she already felt closer to the Right-Unders than to some kids she'd known all her life. There was something about that tree house. . . . It somehow stripped away the superficial stuff. As she settled into bed that night, Tricia reflected on how much she'd learned about her new friends in such a short time. She'd had to unlearn some things, too. She'd thought she had the girls pretty much sized up after the first couple of meetings, but she'd been wrong in a lot of ways. She reached for her Right-Under journal and began writing:

Elizabeth isn't a babyish little kid. She may be the smartest one in the club.
Mei is quiet, but she really knows who she is.
Sometimes Hope's sense of humor is a cover for sadness.
Leighton isn't nearly as pulled together as she wants everybody to believe.

Tricia read over the list, rubbing her eyes sleepily. These girls really had become friends. They didn't just help each other . . . they knew each other. Tricia laid the journal on her bedside table, turned off her lamp and lay quietly as her eyelids fluttered in the darkness.

19

Tricia felt unusually lazy for the next few days. The weather matched her mood. The persistent summer sunshine had given way to a three-day stretch of misty rain. The temperature was still warm, but the gray sky made Tricia feel chilly. She stayed in her room and read a lot.

But just as she'd get to a good part in the book, she would find her attention wandering. She didn't even realize it until she turned the page and realized she couldn't remember a word she'd just read. That wasn't like her. She was usually so focused.

Everly occasionally toddled in, shoving a picture book under Tricia's nose or ordering her to play, but Tricia waved her away.

Late Wednesday afternoon, Tricia gave up on her book and plopped onto her bed. She lazily outlined the planets on her bedspread with her finger. She was glad the Right-Unders were meeting the next day. She needed the company. And yet . . .

All the girls had shared a problem except her. Mei's mural . . . Hope's spa day . . . Elizabeth's visit with her grandparents . . . Leighton's cousin's wedding . . .

Tricia was much more comfortable hearing other people's

problems than sharing her own. But she knew the girls wouldn't let her off the hook.

Why did she think it would be so difficult? The Right-Unders would surely understand. After all, their "complicated" families had led them to form the club. But Tricia's family seemed somehow more complicated than the others. True, Hope's mom and Leighton's dad had fallen off the face of the earth, but at least everybody was clear on the matter. Tricia's relationships—well, one relationship in particular—seemed fuzzier. How could she make the girls understand? She didn't even understand it herself.

She laid her cheek against Jupiter and breathed in the fragrance of the freshly laundered spread. Like it or not, it was time to give the Right-Unders a chance to help her.

• • •

"The July fifteenth meeting of the Right-Under club is now in session."

Tricia tapped the Problem Stick against the floor of the tree house.

Hope looked at her knowingly.

"What?" Tricia asked defensively.

"It's your turn," Hope said.

Tricia fingered the Problem Stick nervously. "Old business?" she said weakly.

Hope shook her head. "We covered old business during our emergency meeting. It's time for us to help you with your problem."

"What if I don't have a problem?"

"We know that's what you want everybody to believe,"

Hope said. "But we know better. Just because you're our oh-so-wise leader doesn't mean you don't need help, too."

Tricia blushed. The Right-Unders really did know her.

"Spill it," Leighton said tersely, and everyone laughed, relieved to see their friend back in familiar form.

Tricia chewed her bottom lip.

"Okay," she said. "I'll tell you my problem. But I don't think you'll be able to help."

Hope dropped her jaw in mock indignation. "What do we look like, chopped liver?"

Tricia grinned. "Okay, okay."

She stared down at her hands as she rubbed them together. "It's my dad," she blurted out.

"Nooo!" Hope said sarcastically, and the others laughed.

Tricia shrugged. "See? That's just the thing. You already know I miss my dad, but there's nothing anybody can do about it."

"Why?" Elizabeth asked. "Why can't you see him more often?"

Tricia's mouth tightened. "I don't know," she said. "I think my mom is totally jealous of my relationship with him. It's so weird. . . . It's like she has this cut-and-paste idea about families: cut my dad out, paste Troy in. Troy's okay, but he's not my dad, and my mom can't make me stop loving my real dad."

"Your mom doesn't seem like the type who would want to bust up your relationship with your dad," Hope said sensibly. The others nodded.

"Then why won't she let me spend more time with him?" Tricia asked angrily. "I only get to see him once or twice a month, and then just for a quick hamburger or bowling. Mom even sits in the parking lot while I'm with him."

"She sits in the parking lot?" Mei asked incredulously.

Tricia nodded. "She tells me she's going shopping or whatever, but I know she's right outside. She just can't stand the thought of me having a little time with my dad. And God forbid I ask to spend the night with him."

"Well . . . ," Elizabeth said. "Have you asked?"

Tricia looked exasperated. "Of course I have. I ask all the time. I beg Mom to let me spend a weekend with my dad. But the answer is always no, and she never has a good reason. She just gets him on the phone, then runs me over to McDonald's for a half-hour visit." She twirled her finger in the air sarcastically, surprising herself by feeling an urge to cry. "It's not enough." Her voice broke.

Her words hung in the air for a tense moment. It was odd seeing Tricia like this. She was usually so . . . in charge.

"Tricia, your mom is utterly reasonable," Mei said. "You just need to talk to her."

"I told you, I've tried," Tricia snapped. "She may seem great to you guys, but trust me, she is totally off the wall where my dad is concerned. He says so himself. And she can hardly ever be bothered with my problems anyway. It's all about Troy and Neverly. I'm a distant third. Very distant."

Mei looked unconvinced. "I just don't see it," she said.

"Some things you can only know firsthand," Hope said supportively. "After all, everybody besides me thinks Jacie is great."

"I don't hear anybody talking about how great my stepdad is," Mei said with a smile.

"He's the principal," Hope said. "Principals have no shot at greatness. Sorry."

Tricia twirled a lock of her blond hair. "My mom's okay," she concluded. "She just doesn't get it. And she definitely doesn't get my dad."

"What's he like?" Mei asked.

"Totally cool," Tricia said, warming to the subject. "He wears his hair in a ponytail. His jeans have holes in the knees."

"O*kay*," Leighton said.

"He's just totally comfortable with himself, you know?" Tricia explained. "He doesn't care what other people think. He plays the guitar and writes his own songs. He's a poet."

Hope wrinkled her brow. "Does he make any money at it?"

Tricia rolled her eyes. "It's not about money. It's about following your heart. I love Mom, but we have nothing in common. I wish I could live with Dad."

Wow. That was the first time she'd ever said that out loud.

"That's no good," Hope replied. "Then you wouldn't live here, and where would we meet?"

Tricia ran her finger along the bark of the Problem Stick. "I figured you wouldn't be able to help me." She smiled at her friends. "But thanks for trying."

"Not so fast," Hope said. "We haven't written down our solutions yet, and mine is going to be brilliant. Not that I've thought of it yet . . ."

"Hope's right," Elizabeth said. "Get your notebooks ready, everybody. It's time to write down our solutions."

Tricia appreciated their efforts, but she felt so self-conscious . . . so exposed. Why hadn't she made up some lame problem like hating her mom's cooking or something? Her relationship with her dad felt so special, so exclusive. She loved her friends, but she liked keeping her dad all to herself. Now she'd spilled her guts, and there was no turning back.

She glanced at her watch and said, "Your five minutes starts . . . now."

The girls scribbled quickly, then erased, then scribbled some more. Most of them could have written entire essays on the "I Miss My Dad" theme. Mei thought about hers . . . the college professor with close-cropped hair and a serious expression. Her mom told her how much her dad had loved bouncing her in the air and "flying" her like a plane. Mei couldn't remember any of it, of course, but she was glad she had lighthearted stories to balance the sternness he projected in his pictures. He had been brilliant, too . . . a scientist. Mei knew he would have done great things if he had lived. She wished she'd known him.

Leighton couldn't remember her father, either, even though he was alive and well. He was her mom's high school sweetheart . . . a football player with muscular arms, narrow hips and dimples in his cheeks. She got her thick dark hair and olive complexion from him. He had freaked when Leighton's mom told him shortly before high school graduation that she was pregnant. He turned nasty, calling her mom mean names and questioning whether the baby was even his. Her mom had never seen that side of him before, probably because she'd never seen him scared before. After all, he was just a kid. Leighton's mother had understood, but it hadn't made the heartache any easier when her boyfriend abruptly moved out of town with his family. She had tried to maintain contact, and a couple of times, he had even stopped by to see the baby. But Leighton was nothing to him except a grim reminder of his teenage stupidity. He had moved on with his life. Leighton wasn't part of it.

It had been tough for Leighton's mother. She'd managed to coax a few child-support payments from him, but the money was nothing she could count on, barely enough to pay for a couple of boxes of diapers. She was on her own and she knew it.

She'd scrapped her dream of being an architect and gotten an entry-level job at a hospital. Eventually, she had worked her way up to becoming a medical transcriptionist, but money was always tight. She'd worked so hard, and she'd used her vacation time to haul schoolchildren around on field trips and bring cupcakes to Leighton's class for special occasions. She must have been tired most of the time, and she'd never had any money for herself, but she'd never, ever complained. She'd just put one foot in front of the other. Then she had met Carl. . . .

Elizabeth's dad . . . well, it was impossible not to think of dads when concentrating on a solution for Tricia, but Elizabeth had gotten very good at pushing him out of her thoughts. It was too painful to compare the old dad with the new dad. He'd been so funny and fun-loving until last year. Now he was bitter and angry. Her mom, too. It was as if aliens had inhabited their bodies. All they did was scream at each other, then stomp around stewing. They tried to keep things civil for Elizabeth's sake, but emotions ran too high. They were both so hurt. Elizabeth didn't know all the details, but she was all too attuned to the shrill accusations and slamming doors. Why couldn't they just take a deep breath and stop destroying the family? That was how she felt sometimes: destroyed. When she thought about it. And she thought about it as seldom as possible.

"Time's up."

Tricia's voice interrupted their thoughts. Tricia blushed and pulled a lock of hair behind her ear.

"I guess it's time for you to fix my life," she said.

She passed the bowl around as the girls folded their pieces of paper twice and dropped them in.

"Can I read the solutions this time?" Elizabeth asked.

"Sure," Leighton responded. "It's your turn."

My turn, Elizabeth thought. She liked the sound of that.

She reached for the bowl, unfolded the papers and read them one by one:

"SOLUTION: Sit down with both your mom AND your dad at the same time and tell them how you feel. If your parents are like mine, you probably get one story from your mom and another story from your dad. If you're all in the same room together, everybody will have to come clean.

"SOLUTION: Remind your mom that if you spend every other weekend with your dad, you'll be out of her hair for a while and she'll have Troy and Neverly all to herself.

"SOLUTION: Ask your dad for guitar lessons so you'll have an excuse to see him more often. Your mom probably won't mind because you'll be doing something productive.

"SOLUTION: Quit stressing about your dad. Dads are highly overrated."

As Elizabeth set the bowl on the floor, Leighton leaned back onto the palms of her hands. "Dads really are overrated," she mused, more to herself than to anyone else.

"Hmmm. Wonder which solution was yours," Hope teased.

"I think the guitar lessons are a really good idea," Elizabeth said, then quickly added, "and that wasn't my solution."

"Mom would never go for it," Tricia said.

"Why not?" Mei asked. "Doesn't every mom want her kid to take music lessons?"

"Not from him," Tricia muttered, staring down at her hands.

"But you said he's a really good guitarist . . . right?" Mei persisted.

"It's just not a good idea!"

Tricia spoke so sharply that the words hung in the air. A knot tightened in her stomach. She hated this, having her deepest feelings picked over like grapefruits in the produce department of a grocery store. She couldn't explain why she missed her dad so much . . . she just did. She couldn't explain why her mom hated how close Tricia was to her dad . . . she just did. Tricia didn't understand any of it. She just felt it. She was embarrassed to create so much tension in the room but suddenly resented the girls' intrusiveness. She didn't want to talk to them about her dad, and she certainly wasn't interested in their lame solutions. Maybe this whole club had been a stupid idea.

"Tricia," Mei said gently, "nobody can really understand your problem except you. But that's true for all of us, you know."

"So what are you saying?" Tricia asked angrily. "That I think I'm all that because my problem is extra special? I don't think it's extra special. I think it extra sucks."

"If you won't let us try to help you, maybe you're just happier being miserable," Leighton said with an arched eyebrow.

Okay, that was it. "This is a stupid club," Tricia muttered. She stomped out of the tree house.

20

Tricia moped in her house all that day and the next. She would hole up in her room for an hour or two, then wander into the den and click the television's remote control a few times, then go into the kitchen and peer into the pantry. Nothing looked good. She wasn't hungry anyway.

"What's wrong, honey?" her mom asked her as Tricia roamed restlessly through the kitchen that Friday evening.

Tricia shrugged.

"You've been so quiet the last couple of days," her mom said, wiping off the kitchen counter. She walked over to Tricia. "Is something wrong?"

Tricia hadn't planned to say anything, but the words spilled out: "I want to see my dad."

Her mother subtly sucked in her breath. "He said . . . he could probably take you bowling . . . next Saturday," she said haltingly.

"I don't want to go bowling!" Tricia spat. "I don't want to do anything with him. I just want to be with him. For longer than fifteen minutes! And without you waiting outside in the parking lot!"

Tricia's mother bit her bottom lip. "Honey . . . ," she began.

"I've heard it all before!" Tricia cried, flinging her hands in the air. " 'Dad's so busy.' 'I don't like you spending the night away from home.' 'This is your family now.' Well, you know what? You can't wish Dad away, no matter how hard you try. And why do you try? Don't I deserve to have my dad?"

"Honey . . ." Her mom tried to touch her arm, but Tricia jerked it away.

"I don't want to hear anything else you have to say!" she screamed at her mother through tears that were now flowing freely. "I've listened to you for the last time!"

• • •

The idea formed so effortlessly that Tricia considered it destiny. Of course she would do it. Why hadn't she thought of it before? It wasn't like she was a kid anymore; she'd be thirteen in three more weeks. She didn't have to run to her mother for every little thing. Her mother would probably be relieved that Tricia was finally taking matters into her own hands. That was part of growing up, right?

She even had her own money. She wasn't sure how much it would cost, but she had been saving babysitting money from watching Hissy on occasional afternoons and evenings. She hadn't had any particular goal in mind; she just liked the thought of money in her pocket. Now she knew why. Destiny.

Still, guilt nagged at her. She reached over to her bedside table for her Right-Under journal. There were plenty of good reasons to carry out her plan. She wrote them down:

I'll be home by Sunday night, and I'll call Mom so she won't worry. She'll understand.

I've tried asking for her help. She refuses, so what choice do I have?

Like one of the Right-Unders said, she'll get to have her "real" family all to herself for a change. I'm doing Mom a favor.

Dad will be so psyched by my visit that he'll insist on seeing me every weekend. Mom won't be able to bully him—or me—anymore.

There were plenty more good reasons, but these were enough to assuage Tricia's guilt. She put her journal back on her bedside table and turned off her lamp.

• • •

Tricia had been silly to worry she would oversleep. Actually, she had barely slept at all . . . just tossed and turned. By six o'clock that morning, she was pulling on her jeans and her R.U. T-shirt. She was embarrassed about lashing out at the girls and hoped they weren't mad at her. But she'd have lots to report at the next meeting, and for now, she needed the symbol of moral support. She glanced at the clock on her bedside table: 6:04. She'd have plenty of time to be out the door before the rest of the family woke up.

She retrieved a wad of cash—forty-two dollars—from her jewelry box and pulled her hair into a ponytail. Then she brushed her teeth, tossed a change of clothes into an overnight bag and crept downstairs to the kitchen.

She slowly opened a drawer to keep it from creaking, then pulled out the phone book. It wasn't totally pathetic that she didn't know her dad's address; he moved around a lot and hadn't been in his new apartment long. Just a few months . . . a year tops. She flipped through the pages of the phone book, reached the Hs, then followed the list of names with her index finger.

"Harper . . . Hathaway . . . Hayden."

That was it.

"Hayden, Anthony . . . Hayden, Charles . . . Hayden, Patrick."

She sighed with relief. There was her dad: "Patrick Hayden: 116 Drawbridge Road, Apartment 3-C."

Should she call him first? Nah . . . she wouldn't risk any obstacles.

Now that she had her dad's address, she flipped back to the yellow pages. What would the listing be, taxis or cabs? She tried cabs. No luck. She flipped more pages. Aaah . . . "taxicabs." The first listing would do.

She called and heard one ring, then two, then five, six, seven. . . . She was just about to hang up when a bored voice said, "A-1 Taxi Service. May I help you?"

Tricia cleared her throat and smoothed her T-shirt. "Um . . ."

"Can you speak up, please?"

"Um . . . I need a cab ride, please, to 116 Drawbridge Road."

Tricia heard the operator typing information into a computer. "And where does the driver pick you up?" she asked.

Tricia's mind blanked. Your address, she told herself wryly. Not a difficult question. "1445 Adamsville Road," she said. "In the Cross Creek subdivision."

More clacking keys. Then, "A driver will be there in about ten minutes."

Whew. Now there was no turning back.

Tricia inched the kitchen door open, gently closed it behind her and went to her driveway to wait for her ride. A breeze brushed her face and birds sang in the trees. In ten minutes, she'd be on her way to her dad's apartment. This was so cool. "So cool." She said it out loud. So she'd believe it.

• • •

"*How* much?"

Tricia had had no idea how much a cab ride would cost, but eighteen dollars was beyond the farthest reaches of her imagination.

"Eighteen bucks," the driver repeated blandly, nodding at the meter.

Tricia pulled a twenty out of her jeans pocket and smoothed it. She handed it to the driver, who began to put it in his pocket.

"Don't I get two dollars back?" she asked.

He cocked his head in her direction. "Unless you'd like to . . . oh, I don't know . . . maybe give me a tip like people usually do."

Tricia blushed. "Sure, of course."

She grasped her overnight bag and got out of the car. A couple of people were getting into their cars in the parking lot, but otherwise, the apartment complex was still and hushed. A wave of panic welled in Tricia's throat. What was she doing here? Her dad might not even be home. This was nuts.

But she swallowed hard. Why should it be such a big deal to go see her dad? Why was she freaking out? He'd be thrilled to see her. He told her repeatedly that if it wasn't for her mom, they'd be together all the time. Now she was old enough to make it happen, with or without her mother's cooperation. Still . . . this felt so weird.

Tricia walked from the parking lot to the C building of

the complex. The paint on the apartment doors was dingy and crumbling. The iron numbers on the doors were badly rusted; the two hung upside down. Oh, well. That meant Dad's was next.

Tricia stood in front of 3-C and took a deep breath.

"He's probably asleep, stupid," she said out loud. But here she was. She pressed the doorbell. Nothing. Maybe it didn't work. She hadn't heard it from outside. She pressed again. Nothing.

She knocked, gently at first . . . *tap, tap, tap*. Still nothing. She knocked harder, then harder, then started pounding on the door with her fist. She felt like crying. This was so stupid. Why hadn't she asked the cab driver to wait for her? That way, she could have gone straight home and pondered her forty-dollar mistake. Stupid, stupid.

"Tricia?"

The door was flung open and there stood Tricia's dad in tattered jeans and a faded T-shirt, scratching his beard and peering out at her.

"Hey, Dad."

Nobody was nervous around their own dad, right? So why was she so nervous?

"What are you doing here?" Her dad's soft blue eyes squinted in bewilderment.

Tricia shrugged, aiming for nonchalant. "Just felt like dropping by."

"Dropping by?"

Her heart sank. Was he even going to let her in?

"Oh . . . ," he said, stepping back from the door as if reading her mind. "Come in, sweetie, come in."

Tricia walked in and wrinkled her nose at a musty, sour

smell. A tattered plaid chair sat in one corner of the room, dad's guitar propped against it. A card table with a wobbly . stood in the adjoining dining area, with one metal chair pushe under it. That was all the furniture she saw. Newspapers and magazines were strewn everywhere. A couple of coffee cups were on the floor, one on its side. It was the one she had given him for Christmas: "World's Greatest Dad."

Her father still looked stunned, but he opened his arms expansively. "So," he said sheepishly, "this is my place."

"Furniture is highly overrated," Tricia said.

He laughed, but he looked troubled. "Does your mom know you're here?"

"Yeah . . ." Tricia couldn't believe how easily she had just lied.

Her dad's eyes narrowed. "She does?"

She nodded quickly but couldn't look at him. "What's the big deal?" she asked defensively. "Like I said, I just thought I'd drop by . . . maybe spend the weekend."

Panic flooded her father's face. "The weekend?"

Tricia laced her fingers together anxiously. "Just the two of us." Her voice was barely a whisper.

"That sounds sensational, sweetie, but . . . Did I know you were coming?"

"It's a surprise," she said, then impulsively kissed him on the cheek. "Can't a daughter surprise her dad?"

Her voice was light, but her heart was sinking. This didn't feel right. Why not? A daughter should be able to surprise her dad with an unscheduled visit. But then, a daughter should also know where her dad lives without having to check the phone book.

"Sweetie, I'm not exactly set up for guests," her dad said, squeezing his chin nervously.

"Guests?"

That was what Tricia was—a guest. And an unwelcome one, at that.

"You know . . ." Her dad waved his arm apologetically. "I haven't had time yet to do much with the place."

Tricia took a deep breath. "Dad, just chill," she said decisively. "I don't need furniture. I just want to hang out with you." Her eyes wandered. She spotted the guitar, then remembered the Right-Under solution.

"Why don't you teach me how to play the guitar?" she suggested, willing herself to relax.

Her dad shook his head, as if trying to dislodge the goofy thoughts tumbling around in his brain. "You're sure your mother knows you're here?"

"Duh, Dad. Are you going to spend our whole visit giving me the third degree? You're always telling me how you wish we could spend more time together. Well, here I am." She held out her palms as if offering proof.

"Okay then," he said slowly, brushing a hand through his unkempt shoulder-length hair. "I don't usually give guitar lessons at five a.m. on Saturday mornings. . . ."

"It's almost seven," Tricia corrected him.

"Right. Seven." He tossed his hands in the air. "Sounds like the perfect time for a guitar lesson. Let me just . . . I don't know . . . freshen up a little."

He disappeared down a hallway and she sat in the sole chair in his living room. He came back smelling of toothpaste, his hair pulled into a loose ponytail.

"Where will you sit?" she asked him.

"My favorite spot." He plopped on the floor beside her and cradled the guitar. "Okay," he said, his voice mildly shaky, "the first thing you need to know is: Every Boy Gets Donuts and Eggs."

Tricia's brow knitted. "What?"

"Every Boy Gets Donuts and Eggs. Those are the notes a guitar is tuned to: E, B, G, D, A and E, starting from the bottom."

He plucked the strings one by one, naming them as he went along.

"Why isn't it tuned to A, B, C, D, E and F?" Tricia asked.

Her dad smiled. "Because then there would be no need to memorize Every Boy Gets Donuts and Eggs."

"Speaking of donuts and eggs," Tricia said, "I didn't have breakfast before I left the house. I'm kinda starved."

Her dad looked panicked again, even a little irritated. "Sweetie, I told you, I don't have much food. If I'd known you were coming . . ."

"Fine, fine," she said. "Just keep teaching me."

"Well . . . I might have some soda," he said. "Give me just a second and I'll see what I can find."

He stood up and walked into the kitchen. Tricia heard him rustling around in the cupboard and refrigerator. He came back a moment later with two glasses. He handed one to Tricia and she took a sip. Coke.

"My kinda breakfast," she said.

He returned to the floor, placing his glass at his side.

"We'll start with a few basic chords," he said, settling the guitar back on his lap.

Tricia couldn't help smiling. She loved the serene expression on her dad's face when he played the guitar. It brought back a million memories of him singing her to sleep. He was the coolest dad ever . . . even if he didn't have any furniture. Maybe even because he didn't have any furniture.

She watched closely as he showed her where to put her fingers; then she put her glass on the floor and took the guitar from him. Following his directions, she placed a finger on the third fret of the high E string, then strummed from the D string down.

"G," her dad said.

"Gee?" Tricia repeated, puzzled.

"G. The G chord. You just learned your first chord."

Tricia grinned. "Teach me more."

They sat there for another hour or so. Tricia's fingertips on her left hand were sore from pressing the strings, but she wasn't about to say so. She was even getting used to the musty, sour smell, a smell that was replaced with a smoky odor when her dad emerged from the bathroom.

"Were you smoking in there?" she asked him, more playfully than probingly.

"Promise me you'll never smoke, Tricia," he responded without answering her question. "It'll kill you."

"Promise," she said. Now that the awkward tension of her unannounced entrance was over, Tricia was savoring her dad's company. She loved seeing his world. It wasn't exactly neat or orderly, but it was his.

She was practicing more chords when he refilled their glasses and sat back down beside her. "You know, I wrote a song about you," he said.

Tricia beamed. "Play it for me."

He hesitated, but then took the guitar from her, cradled it in his lap, closed his eyes and sang,

"The first time that I saw her, her eyes, they said it all.
They said, 'You're my whole wide world, so will you catch me when I fall?
'And will you sing me songs and will you keep me warm at night?
'And when the thunder rumbles, will you please just hold me tight?' "

Tricia closed her eyes and swayed.

"In Patricia's eyes, I'm brave and wise, and I'm stronger than the sea.
Oh, I wish that I could somehow be what my daughter sees in me.
In Patricia's eyes, I can realize all my wildest hopes and dreams.
Am I what I seem to be in Patricia's eyes?"

Stillness filled the air as he sang the last word. Tricia didn't want the moment to end. She was still swaying, willing this moment to last. But she opened her eyes when she heard her father sniffling. He was wiping a tear from his eye.

"Dad?"

He forced a smile. "I just love you so much, honey. I really do."

"I love you, too, Dad," she said with a sense of urgency. Thoughts tumbled in her head. Maybe I could live with you! We could play the guitar together every day! There's no reason for us to go whole weeks without seeing each other! I want my dad back. Please?

Her dad took a drink from his glass, then held it in front of him. "A toast," he said, "to the new guitarist in the family."

21

Three hours and five trips to the refrigerator later, Tricia and her dad were still playing the guitar. By now, Tricia was hungry and exhausted.

"Dad," she said, laying the guitar aside, "I think I need a break."

Silence.

"Dad?"

She glanced over at him. His eyes were closed. He was still sitting upright, but his head was bobbing slightly.

"Dad?" Tricia said.

The phone rang. Her dad didn't budge. Tricia sat there anxiously, not sure what to do. After the fifth ring, the answering machine picked up. Tricia heard her dad's jovial recorded greeting, then a familiar voice.

"Patrick, are you there? Patrick, pick up. Please!"

Tricia's heart skipped a beat as she recognized her mom's voice.

"Uh . . . Dad," she said, then nudged her father. His eyes remained closed. "Patrick, please pick up! Tricia is missing!" Her mother's voice broke. "She's missing, Patrick!"

Tricia heard Troy's voice in the background.

Oh, no. . . . What had she done? Her mother sounded frantic. Tricia had never heard her that way before. She always seemed so . . . in control.

Tricia looked down at her dad. His eyes were still closed and his head had slumped to one side. She nudged him harder.

"Dad! Dad, wake up!"

Tricia's mom begged Patrick to return her call, then hung up. Tricia felt desperate to see her mom. How could she have done this to her?

"*Dad!*" Tricia shook him roughly.

His eyelids parted into tiny slits.

"Dad, wake up!" Tricia shouted.

His raised his eyebrows, but his eyes were still barely open.

"Dad, that was Mom on the phone," Tricia said breathlessly. "I lied to you. I didn't tell her I was coming. She's really worried. I have to get home, Dad. Now."

He stared at her with glassy eyes.

"Now, Dad!" Tricia begged.

She got out of the chair and pulled his arms. He slowly rose to his feet, then staggered for a moment.

"Wha . . . ," he said.

"Get your keys," Tricia commanded. "You have to take me home. Now."

He nodded but still looked disoriented. Tricia spotted the keys on the card table in the dining area. She grabbed them and stuffed them in his hand. "Let's go, Dad."

"Right," her father responded groggily. "Time to go."

• • •

"Dad, pay attention! You're weaving."

Patrick's head bobbed erratically as he drove Tricia home. He was driving so slowly . . . ridiculously slowly. All Tricia wanted was to get home. In ten minutes, she'd be where she belonged. Ten minutes. Hurry, Dad, hurry, she thought.

"Thank you for coming to see me, baby," her dad said, slurring his words.

"You're welcome," Tricia replied tersely, looking straight ahead as if willing the car to get her home.

"You're my girl . . . you know that, don't you?"

She rolled her eyes. She usually loved it when her dad told her that kind of thing. Now she just felt so impatient to get home.

"You know that, don't you, Tricia?" he repeated loudly.

"Watch the road, Dad!" Tricia barked. He was scaring her.

"You know I love you. I love you more than anything. You know that, don't you, baby?" her father said, leaning his face toward hers.

But Tricia didn't hear him. She was too fixated on the car in front of them.

"Dad . . . *Dad!*"

She managed to spit a piece of shattered glass from her mouth before falling unconscious.

• • •

"Baby?"

Tricia groggily opened her eyes. Everything was blurry. Where was she? And why did she hurt so badly?

"It's okay, baby. You're okay now."

The voice was her mother's. Tricia felt cool fingers gently running through her hair.

"Mom?"

"Yes, sweetie. I'm right here."

Tricia strained to focus her eyes, but the fog remained. "Where am I?"

"You're in the hospital, honey. But you're fine. You're gonna be fine."

Tricia saw a couple of figures bustling about. One approached her and fiddled with her hand. Tricia touched the hand and felt something plastic coming out of it.

"Try not to touch," the figure said. "We need to keep the medicine flowing."

"Am I sick?" Tricia asked through swollen lips. She tasted dried blood on her teeth.

"You had a little accident," the figure said. "But we're taking good care of you. I'm one of your nurses. My name is Sophie. You're gonna be good as new before you know it."

Tricia heard sniffling. She moved her head in that direction, then moaned in pain. But worse than the pain was discovering the source of the sniffling. Her mother was crying.

"Don't cry, Mom," she begged.

Her mom's eyes sparkled. "They're happy tears," she whispered. "I'm just so thankful you're okay."

Tricia groaned. It was all coming back to her now. She was here because she had lied to everybody, gone to her dad's house, worried her mother sick and trusted her stupid dad. Her dad . . .

"Is Dad okay?"

Her mother nodded. "He's fine."

"Where is he?"

Her mother hesitated. "Here for now," she said cautiously. "He's in a room right down the hall. He's okay, I promise. You're in much worse shape than he is." Her mother sounded bitter.

"Was he drunk? Is that why he wrecked the car? He was drinking something, but I thought it was Coke." Tricia closed her eyes, yet her focus was sharpening. What an idiot she was.

"We're not sure if he was drinking, sweetie. They're running some tests." Her mother's face tightened into a pinched expression. "Why did you go there, Tricia?"

Tricia tried to lick her lips, but her tongue was parched. "I just wanted to see him. I'm so sorry, Mom."

Tears trickled down her mother's cheeks. "You never have to apologize for loving your dad."

Tricia's lids felt heavy, but somehow, she felt strong. "I don't love him. I hate him."

Her mother shook her head. "Don't say that. He's your dad, and he loves you. He didn't mean to hurt you, honey, I promise you. He just can't help himself right now."

"Is he an alcoholic?"

Her mom nodded. "Yeah. He drank a lot when he was younger, but he stopped when we got married and stayed sober for years. You kept him sober. He loves you so much. And he was a good dad when he was well."

"Why did he start drinking again?" Tricia asked.

Her mother shook her head slowly. "I don't know, honey. I think he's just really sick. He tries to stay sober, you know. He's always trying. For your sake." She clasped Tricia's finger. "Do you want to see him?"

Tricia pondered her answer. "Maybe later," she said. "Right now, I'd rather see Troy."

• • •

Troy's eyes looked kind as he gingerly held Tricia's hand.

"Why does Everly get a good dad and I'm stuck with a loser?" she asked him sleepily, fighting to keep her eyes open.

"You have a good dad," Troy said, smoothing her hair. "He's just struggling right now."

Tricia loved him for saying that.

"And you've got me, too," Troy continued. "You and Everly are both my girls."

"I'm really stupid, aren't I?" she said.

"No, honey," Troy responded. "You just love your dad. And you should. My dad was an alcoholic, too, but I never stopped loving him."

"My dad's problem . . . I didn't know," Tricia said. "I didn't even know."

Troy nodded. "Your mom didn't want you to. She's always tried really hard to protect you."

"Still . . . you guys should've told me."

Troy shrugged. "Probably so, honey. You can never keep a secret like that for long. Kids have a way of knowing things, even when nobody tells them. I know that from firsthand experience. And as smart as you are . . . you're right, we probably should have told you. But your mom did what she thought was best. She loves you very much, Tricia."

Tap, tap, tap.

Tricia glanced toward the knock on the door of her hospital room. Her mom poked her head in. "Sorry to disturb you two, but you have a surprise visitor if you're up for it, Tricia."

Tricia looked curious. "Who is it?"

Her mom held the door open wider, and in walked Mei.

"Mei!"

Tricia's elation was indescribable. She was so happy to see her friend, someone familiar and comforting, a symbol of everything Tricia loved about her life . . . a fellow Right-Under.

"Hi," Mei said, walking toward Tricia with deep concern in her almond-shaped eyes.

"How did you know I was here?" Tricia asked.

Mei smiled. "I didn't. I saw your mom in the hall."

"But . . . what are you doing in a hospital?"

Mei's lips parted to form a wide smile. "My mom had her baby a couple of hours ago. Tricia, I'm a sister!"

Tricia couldn't resist returning Mei's smile. "Ouch," she said, touching her fingertips to her swollen mouth. "Mei, that's great."

"He came a few weeks early, but he's six pounds and totally healthy."

"Wow. A baby brother."

Mei nodded. "His name is Stanley Wu. Stanley after my stepdad, of course. Wu after my mom's dad . . . which was also my dad's name." She tilted her head to one side. "The middle name was Stan's idea."

Tricia grinned mischievously. "That's a seriously awful name, you know."

Mei giggled. "I know. But I'll beat up anybody who teases him about it."

Now, that was a funny image.

"Okay, maybe not," Mei said. "Instead, how about we keep his middle name to ourselves? Right-Under honor?"

Tricia nodded. "Right-Under honor."

But she knew how proud Mei was. And she knew how much fun it was to be a big sister, when it wasn't a total pain in the neck.

"Hey, Troy?" Tricia said, glancing at her stepdad. "I'm dying to see Everly."

22

"The July twenty-second meeting of the Right-Under Club is now in session."

All the girls had visited Tricia in the hospital, then several more times after she'd returned home, but it wasn't until they saw her in the tree house that they knew she really was going to be okay.

"First order of business: to teach our president how to cover up hideous black-and-blue marks with makeup," Leighton teased.

Tricia managed a weak smile. Her swelling was almost gone, but the bruises remained, and she still had stitches over one eye. Her R.U. shirt was torn and stained from the accident, but she wore it proudly.

"No," Tricia corrected Leighton, "the first order of business is to officially welcome our mascot into the club: Mei's new brother, Stanley."

"Hey, Right-Unders have to be girls," Hope pointed out good-naturedly.

"Trust me, he's too busy pooping to make the meetings," Mei said, and everyone laughed. Mei turned toward Tricia. "Besides, we have our hands full with old business. Tricia, as if your bruises don't speak for themselves, you know the drill. Time to report on your problem."

Tricia squeezed the Problem Stick and crossed her legs at the ankles. "As everyone knows, my problem ended with a bang," she said with a grin. "Which means you also know my dad is an alcoholic, which means you also know he's been arrested for driving under the influence, which means you also know my life is in a complete shambles." She shrugged. "But it's okay."

"We should've guessed your mom had a good reason for staying nearby when you were with your dad," Elizabeth said. "Do you hate him?"

Tricia nodded, but her expression was soft. "Yeah. But I love him, too. How's that for weird?"

"Why did you sneak off without telling your mom?" Hope said. "I don't remember that being one of our solutions."

"I was an idiot," Tricia said. "I can't explain it. I kinda felt like his life was a mess, but I needed to see for myself. I thought I could help him."

"When will you see him again?" Elizabeth asked.

"No time soon," Tricia said. "He's in rehab. He insists he's cleaning up his act. I think he's really gonna try. I hope he can pull it off. I know he's pretty pathetic right now, but he's great in a lot of ways . . . you know?"

Hope nodded. "That's how I feel about my mom. But I'm probably just kidding myself."

Tricia lowered her eyes. "I might be kidding myself, too," she said. "But I want to give him the benefit of the doubt." She shrugged. "He's my dad."

"Hey, nobody's perfect," Mei said soothingly. "It's easy for me to pretend my dad was perfect because he's not around anymore. But I'm sure he had plenty of flaws."

"Everybody does," Hope said.

A muted sound of sniffling drew the girls' eyes to Elizabeth.

"Are you crying, Elizabeth?" Tricia asked, leaning in closer.

Elizabeth looked down, wiped an eye and shook her head.

"Yes, you are," Hope said. "What's up?"

Elizabeth covered her face with her hands. They sat there silently for a few moments while she cried.

"You can tell us," Tricia said quietly. "We're Right-Unders. We R There for U. Remember?"

Elizabeth lowered her hands and looked at the girls through moist eyes. "I'm so glad you guys are my friends," she said.

"Is it your grandmother, Elizabeth?" Mei asked. "Has she gotten worse?"

Elizabeth shook her head. "She's about the same. It's really sad, but at least my mom finally knows what's going on. She found a lady who can stay with Grandma when Grandpa's working on the farm. We don't know how long that can last—Grandma's going to keep getting sicker—but at least I don't worry about her as much."

"Then why are you crying?" Hope persisted.

Elizabeth folded her hands and laid them in her lap. "I don't know. . . . You guys talking about your parents is making me think about mine. I'll have to go home soon, wherever that might be."

"What do you mean?" Tricia asked.

Elizabeth took a deep breath. "My parents both want me to live with them. A judge wants me to decide. When I go back, I have to tell the judge where I want to live. She wants it settled before school starts."

The girls shared anxious glances.

"That totally sucks," Leighton said.

"Well, it's not happening!" Hope's voice was so forceful that everyone jumped slightly. "No way am I letting them treat my cousin that way! Elizabeth, you can just stay with us."

Elizabeth smiled gratefully but shook her head. "I have to go back," she said. "I just don't know how to choose one parent over the other."

"I'll talk to your dad," Hope said breathlessly. "I'll have my dad talk to your dad. He'll listen. We'll fix this, I promise."

"What would you say to her dad?" Leighton challenged. " 'Stop wanting your kid to be with you'? She's lucky both of her parents want her so much."

"But no way should she have to choose," Hope said.

Tricia fingered the Problem Stick. "Do you want us to write down some solutions?" she asked Elizabeth.

Elizabeth's lips tightened. "Thanks," she said, "but I think this is something I'm going to have to work out on my own."

"Why not just flip a coin?" Hope said sarcastically. "That makes as much sense as anything else. The judge is nuts. And your parents are nuts for putting you in this position."

"Thanks for caring," Elizabeth said, looking from one face to the next. "And thanks for letting me be in your club. I know you probably didn't want me in it."

"Why would you say that?" Tricia asked.

"You know. . . . I'm a little kid compared to you guys. But you let me in anyway. I've loved being a Right-Under."

"You're making it sound like it's over," Tricia said.

Elizabeth's eyebrows formed an upside-down V. "I go home in a couple of weeks. And we've all had our turn with the Problem Stick."

Leighton *tsk*ed. "It's not like we're going to run out of problems," she said. "And it's not like you can't come back for visits. We should probably make it an official rule that you have to come to meetings at least once a month. That way, your parents will have to keep bringing you back."

Elizabeth smiled. They wanted her to come back.

"What if we all kinda drift apart once school starts?" Hope asked.

"We won't," Tricia said emphatically. "We've come too far together. You don't go through what we've been through and then just walk away from each other."

The girls' expressions were hopeful. They all wanted to believe it. Still, middle school could be so . . . fickle.

"This may have started out as a dumb kids' club," Tricia continued, "but we all know it's turned into something a lot more than that. We owe it to each other to stick together."

"Besides," Mei teased, "we know each other's secrets. There's no unringing a bell."

She remembered how vulnerable she'd felt when she first started confiding in the girls . . . when she first started trusting them. But now, it felt natural, safe, for the Right-Unders to know her so well.

"Right-Unders stick together through thick and thin," Leighton said firmly. "That's all there is to it."

The girls joined hands and nodded. Leighton was right. That was all there was to it.

23

"*Happy birthday to you!*"

Hope leaned close to Mei. "Why don't people settle on a key before they start singing that stupid song?" she asked.

Mei laughed.

"Here we go!" Tricia's mom walked onto the backyard deck holding a rectangular cake ablaze with candles. "Tricia? Elizabeth? You're up."

Her mom placed the cake on the table as Tricia and Elizabeth walked up to blow out the candles. The white frosting was decorated with pink and yellow roses and the words "Happy Birthday, Tricia" and "Come Back Soon, Elizabeth." It had been Tricia's mom's idea to combine Tricia's birthday party with a celebration of Elizabeth's last weekend in town. The girls blew out the candles, then hugged each other as their parents and friends applauded.

"So," Tricia's mom said as she plucked candles out of the cake and licked the frosting off her fingers, "now that summer's almost over and Elizabeth is going back home, do us parents finally get to find out what R.U. stands for?"

The Right-Unders exchanged glances and shook their heads. "No way," Leighton said.

It felt weird to have all the families together. The girls knew so much about them at this point: the persnickety but good-hearted principal, who was gently cradling his newborn son in his arms as dusk blanketed the backyard party in cozy warmth; Mei's mom, sitting by his side looking tired but utterly content; Jacie, the pretty stepmom who never managed to say quite the right thing to Hope, despite her best intentions; Hope's dad, who had his arm around his daughter's shoulder and occasionally tugged affectionately at her ringlets; Leighton's extra-friendly mom and extra-quiet stepdad, whose eyes sparkled when they looked at each other; Leighton's stepbrother, Kyle, who hung back from the group but looked like he was enjoying himself; Everly, whose face was already smeared with frosting; and Tricia's mom and stepdad, who seemed more relaxed than Tricia had seen them in a long time.

Then there were the surprise visitors: Elizabeth's parents. They stood on opposite ends of the deck but kept smiles plastered on their faces and hovered protectively around their daughter.

"Cross your fingers that they keep behaving themselves," Elizabeth whispered to Tricia as slices of cake were passed around the crowd.

"They both seem really nice," Tricia said. "And they're here together. That's a good sign."

"I think everything's gonna be okay," Elizabeth said. "When they got here this morning, they told me they've been working all summer with . . . with . . . it's called a meditator or something like that."

"Mediator," Elizabeth's dad said, leaning into the conversation and winking at his startled daughter, who hadn't known he was listening.

"Dad!" Elizabeth scolded.

"Okay, okay! No more eavesdropping." He took several steps backward and sat on a bench built into the deck.

Tricia took a bite of her cake with a plastic fork. "What's a mediator?" she asked.

"Somebody who helps keep things fair and friendly during a divorce," Elizabeth responded. "Mom says I won't have to talk to a judge after all, and she and Dad are getting along a lot better. They're working things out so that I can spend time with both of them. They're both getting new houses, but they'll be close by, and I won't have to change schools."

"That's great," Tricia said. "We didn't have to solve your problem; your folks did it for you."

"Yeah." Elizabeth smoothed her R.U. T-shirt. All the girls were wearing them. Solidarity.

"Things are going good for me, too," Tricia said. "My dad's doing great in rehab. I know it may not last, but his counselors say they've never seen anybody more motivated to get sober. My mom and I are going to visit next weekend and have some kind of family counseling session."

"Will he go to jail?" Elizabeth asked.

"Mom says probably not, if he finishes rehab and keeps his probation officer happy." Tricia wrinkled her nose. "I didn't even know what a probation officer was before the wreck. I'm learning more than I ever wanted to know about . . . what do they call it? . . . substance abuse. Such is life with a flawed father."

"Did someone call for a father?" The girls turned toward the voice. It was Mei's stepdad, walking up behind them with little Stanley Wu in his arms.

"He's so cute," Elizabeth cooed, touching the baby's soft head.

"He looks just like Mei did when she was a baby," Mei's mother said, walking over to join them.

"No way," Mei called from the opposite side of the deck. "Stanley's got chronic bed head. No offense, little guy." She smiled at Kyle, who had just brought her a soft drink. "Thanks."

"You're welcome," he said. "Hey, Leighton said your mural in the school cafeteria is awesome. I can't wait to see it."

Mei blushed. "It's no big deal."

"That's not what I hear," Kyle said. "Everybody's talking about how talented you are."

"Thanks." Mei's eyelids fluttered. "That's what I always hear about you. You're, like, the smartest guy in school."

Now it was Kyle's turn to blush.

"Please, Mei. His head might explode if you inflate his ego any bigger than it already is," Leighton teased as she walked over.

Kyle smiled. "Trust me, Leighton: you keep my ego firmly in check."

"No need to thank me." The stepsiblings jostled elbows.

"Hey, incidentally," Leighton's mom said, "how's the math tutoring going?"

Hope and Leighton exchanged glances and burst into laughter.

"We got a little sidetracked," Hope explained, "but I promise we'll make up for lost time before school starts."

Crickets chirped as puffy clouds swallowed the day's last slivers of peach and orange sunlight.

"I say nobody gets to open presents until the grown-ups find out what R.U. stands for," Tricia's mom said playfully.

"Relatives Unwelcome?" Elizabeth's dad teased.

"Real Uppity?" Hope's dad tossed out.

"Relationship University?" Leighton's mom suggested.

The girls giggled. Relationship University. That was almost what their summer had felt like.

"Did I guess it?" Leighton's mom asked excitedly.

"No," her daughter answered, "but you're close."

"Oh, we're close!" Tricia's mom said. "Let's keep guessing, guys. I'm sure we'll come up with it sooner or later."

Tricia smiled. "You can try, Mom. But I have to tell you, sometimes an answer is right under your nose and you don't even know it."

A jasmine-scented breeze wafted through the air as the Right-Unders smiled at each other. Here they were, right under the same patio umbrella. Right under the same velvety evening sky. Right where they belonged.

Acknowledgments

I offer my most heartfelt appreciation to Graham, Greg, and Julianne Deriso, who have filled my life with inestimable joy; to my parents, Gregory and Jane Hurley, who have loved, supported, and inspired me every day of my life; to John Hurley, Anne Cook, Cecilia Raville, and Steve Hurley, the finest siblings on earth; to Beth Antoine for vetting my teen-speak; to Mary Deriso, Sylvia Strelec, and the rest of my extended family for their never-ending encouragement; to my treasured friends, too numerous to name but each with such a special place in my heart; to Christyne Simpson, Kent Hannon, and my other fine teachers in West Point, Georgia, and at the University of Georgia, respectively; to Johnny "Sandman" Sands for teaching me everything I know about the newspaper business and therefore most of what I know about good writing and editing; to Sara Crowe for her patience and guidance; to Michelle Poploff and her colleagues at Delacorte Press for their stellar work; and most of all, to my treasured stepson, Graham Deriso III, for inspiring this book.

About the Author

Christine Hurley Deriso likes writing about things that are right under people's noses without anyone much noticing. Her first novel, *Do-Over,* was published by Delacorte Press. She and her husband, Graham, live with their children, Gregory and Julianne, in South Carolina.